As soon as he put on the light, something inside the shower stall said "Yeeeeeek!" in a startled voice.

He turned quickly, to see two wide eyes staring up at him out of a ball of golden fur. Whatever it was, it had a round head and big ears and a vaguely humanoid face with a little snub nose. It was sitting on its haunches, and in that position it was about a foot high. It had two tiny hands with opposing thumbs. He squatted to have a better look at it.

"Hello there, little fellow," he greeted it. "I never saw anything like you before. What are you, anyhow?"

The small creature looked at him seriously and said "Yeek," in a timid voice.

"Why, sure; you're a Little Fuzzy, is what you are."

And LITTLE FUZZY is one of the most charming and exciting science-fiction novels you will ever read.

H. BEAM PIPER

LITTLE FUZZY

ACE SCIENCE FICTION BOOKS
NEW YORK

LITTLE FUZZY

An Ace Science Fiction Book / published by arrangement with
the author

PRINTING HISTORY
Ace edition / 1962
Twelfth printing / December 1986

ISBN: 0-441-48498-0

Ace Science Fiction Books are published by The Berkley Publishing Group,
200 Madison Avenue, New York, New York 10016.
PRINTED IN THE UNITED STATES OF AMERICA

He detested land-prawns. They were horrible things, which, of course, wasn't their fault. More to the point, they were destructive. They got into things at camp; they would try to eat anything. They crawled into machinery, possibly finding the lubrication tasty, and caused jams. They cut into electric insulation. And they got into his bedding, and bit, or rather pinched, painfully. Nobody loved a land-prawn, not even another land-prawn.

This one dodged the thrown flint, scuttled off a few feet and turned, waving its antennae in what looked like derision. Jack reached for his hip again, then checked the motion. Pistol cartridges cost like crazy; they weren't to be wasted in fits of childish pique. Then he reflected that no cartridge fired at a target is really wasted, and that he hadn't done any shooting recently. Stooping again, he picked up another stone and tossed it a foot short and to the left of the prawn. As soon as it was out of his fingers, his hand went for the butt of the long automatic. It was out and the safety off before the flint landed; as the prawn fled, he fired from the hip. The quasi-crustacean disintegrated. He nodded pleasantly.

"Ol' man Holloway's still hitting things he shoots at."

Was a time, not so long ago, when he took his abilities for granted. Now he was getting old enough to have to verify them. He thumbed on the safety and holstered the pistol, then picked up the glove and put it on again.

Never saw so blasted many land-prawns as this summer. They'd been bad last year, but nothing like this. Even the oldtimers who'd been on Zarathustra since the first colonization said so. There'd be some simple explanation, of course; something that would amaze him at his own obtuseness for not having seen it at once. Maybe the abnormally dry weather had something to do with it. Or increase of something they ate, or decrease of natural enemies.

He'd heard that land-prawns had no natural enemies; he questioned that. Something killed them. He'd seen crushed prawn shells, some of them close to his camp. Maybe stamped on by something with hoofs, and then picked clean by insects. He'd ask Ben Rainsford; Ben ought to know.

Half an hour later, the scanner gave him another inter-

7

ruption pattern. He laid it aside and took up the small vi-brohammer. This time it was a large bean, light pink in color. He separated it from its matrix of flint and rubbed it, and instantly it began glowing.

"Ahhh! This is something like it, now!"

He rubbed harder; warmed further on his pipe bowl, it fairly blazed. Better than a thousand sols, he told himself. Good color, too. Getting his gloves off, he drew out the little leather bag from under his shirt, loosening the drawstrings by which it hung around his neck. There were a dozen and a half stones inside, all bright as live coals. He looked at them for a moment, and dropped the new sunstone in among them, chuckling happily.

Victor Grego, listening to his own recorded voice, rubbed the sunstone on his left finger with the heel of his right palm and watched it brighten. There was, he noticed, a boastful ring to his voice—not the suave, unemphatic tone considered proper on a message-tape. Well, if anybody wondered why, when they played that tape off six months from now in Johannesburg on Terra, they could look in the cargo holds of the ship that had brought it across five hundred light-years of space. Ingots of gold and platinum and gadolinium. Furs and biochemicals and brandy. Perfumes that defied synthetic imitation; hardwoods no plastic could copy. Spices. And the steel coffer full of sunstones. Almost all luxury goods, the only really dependable commodities in interstellar trade.

And he had spoken of other things. Veldbeest meat, up seven per cent from last month, twenty per cent from last year, still in demand on a dozen planets unable to produce Terran-type foodstuffs. Grain, leather, lumber. And he had added a dozen more items to the lengthening list of what Zarathustra could now produce in adequate quantities and no longer needed to import. Not fishhooks and boot buckles, either—blasting explosives and propellants, contragravity-field generator parts, power tools, pharmaceuticals, synthetic textiles. The Company didn't need to carry Zarathustra any more; Zarathustra could carry the Company, and itself.

Fifteen years ago, when the Zarathustra Company had sent him here, there had been a cluster of log and prefab

8

huts beside an improvised landing field, almost exactly where this skyscraper now stood. Today, Mallorysport was a city of seventy thousand; in all, the planet had a population of nearly a million, and it was still growing. There were steel mills and chemical plants and reaction plants and machine works. They produced all their own fissionables, and had recently begun to export a little refined plutonium; they had even started producing collapsium shielding.

The recorded voice stopped. He ran back the spool, set for sixty-speed, and transmitted it to the radio office. In twenty minutes, a copy would be aboard the ship that would hyper out for Terra that night. While he was finishing, his communication screen buzzed.

"Dr. Kellogg's screening you, Mr. Grego," the girl in the outside office told him.

He nodded. Her hands moved, and she vanished in a polychromatic explosion; when it cleared, the chief of the Division of Scientific Study and Research was looking out of the screen instead. Looking slightly upward at the showback over his own screen, Victor was getting his warm, sympathetic, sincere and slightly too toothy smile on straight.

"Hello, Leonard. Everything going all right?"

It either was and Leonard Kellogg wanted more credit than he deserved or it wasn't and he was trying to get somebody else blamed for it before anybody could blame him.

"Good afternoon, Victor." Just the right shade of deference about using the first name—big wheel to bigger wheel. "Has Nick Emmert been talking to you about the Big Blackwater project today?"

Nick was the Federation's resident-general; on Zarathustra he was, to all intents and purposes, the Terran Federation Government. He was also a large stockholder in the chartered Zarathustra Company.

"No. Is he likely to?"

"Well, I wondered, Victor. He was on my screen just now. He says there's some adverse talk about the effect on the rainfall in the Piedmont area of Beta Continent. He was worried about it."

"Well, it would affect the rainfall. After all, we drained

9

half a million square miles of swamp, and the prevailing winds are from the west. There'd be less atmospheric moisture to the east of it. Who's talking adversely about it, and what worries Nick?"

"Well, Nick's afraid of the effect on public opinion on Terra. You know how strong conservation sentiment is; everybody's very much opposed to any sort of destructive exploitation."

"Good Lord! The man doesn't call the creation of five hundred thousand square miles of new farmland destructive exploitation, does he?"

"Well, no, Nick doesn't call it that; of course not. But he's concerned about some garbled story getting to Terra about our upsetting the ecological balance and causing droughts. Fact is, I'm rather concerned myself."

He knew what was worrying both of them. Emmert was afraid the Federation Colonial Office would blame him for drawing fire on them from the conservationists. Kellogg was afraid he'd be blamed for not predicting the effects before his division endorsed the project. As a division chief, he had advanced as far as he would in the Company hierarchy; now he was on a Red Queen's race-track, running like hell to stay in the same place.

"The rainfall's dropped ten per cent from last year, and fifteen per cent from the year before that," Kellogg was saying. "And some non-Company people have gotten hold of it, and so has Interworld News. Why, even some of my people are talking about ecological side-effects. You know what will happen when a story like that gets back to Terra. The conservation fanatics will get hold of it, and the Company'll be criticized."

That would hurt Leonard. He identified himself with the Company. It was something bigger and more powerful than he was, like God.

Victor Grego identified the Company with himself. It was something big and powerful, like a vehicle, and he was at the controls.

"Leonard, a little criticism won't hurt the Company," he said. "Not where it matters, on the dividends. I'm afraid you're too sensitive to criticism. Where did Emmert get this story anyhow? From your people?"

"No, absolutely not, Victor. That's what worries him. It was this man Rainsford who started it."

"Rainsford?"

Dr. Bennett Rainsford, the naturalist. Institute of Zeno-Sciences. I never trusted any of those people; they always poke their noses into things, and the Institute always reports their findings to the Colonial Office."

"I know who you mean now; little fellow with red whiskers, always looks as though he'd been sleeping in his clothes. Why, of course the Zeno-Sciences people poke their noses into things, and of course they report their findings to the government." He was beginning to lose patience. "I don't see what all this is about, Leonard. This man Rainsford just made a routine observation of meteorological effects. I suggest you have your meteorologists check it, and if it's correct pass it on to the news services along with your other scientific findings."

"Nick Emmert thinks Rainsford is a Federation undercover agent."

That made him laugh. Of course there were undercover agents on Zarathustra, hundreds of them. The Company had people here checking on him; he knew and accepted that. So did the big stockholders, like Interstellar Explorations and the Banking Cartel and Terra-Baldur-Marduk Spacelines. Nick Emmert had his corps of spies and stool pigeons, and the Terran Federation had people here watching both him and Emmert. Rainsford could be a Federation agent—a roving naturalist would have a wonderful cover occupation. But this Big Blackwater business was so utterly silly. Nick Emmert had too much graft on his conscience; it was too bad that overloaded consciences couldn't blow fuses.

"Suppose he is, Leonard. What could he report on us? We are a chartered company, and we have an excellent legal department, which keeps us safely inside our charter. It is a very liberal charter, too. This is a Class-III uninhabited planet; the Company owns the whole thing outright. We can do anything we want as long as we don't violate colonial law or the Federation Constitution. As long as we don't do that, Nick Emmert hasn't anything to worry about. Now forget this whole damned business, Leonard!" He was beginning to speak sharply, and Kellogg was looking hurt.

11

"I know you were concerned about injurious reports getting back to Terra, and that was quite commendable, but . . ."

By the time he got through, Kellogg was happy again. Victor blanked the screen, leaned back in his chair and began laughing. In a moment, the screen buzzed again. When he snapped it on, his screen-girl said:

"Mr. Henry Stenson's on, Mr. Grego."

"Well, put him on." He caught himself just before adding that it would be a welcome change to talk to somebody with sense.

The face that appeared was elderly and thin; the mouth was tight, and there were squint-wrinkles at the corners of the eyes.

"Well, Mr. Stenson. Good of you to call. How are you?"

"Very well, thank you. And you?" When he also admitted to good health, the caller continued: "How is the globe running? Still in synchronization?"

Victor looked across the office at his most prized possession, the big globe of Zarathustra that Henry Stenson had built for him, supported six feet from the floor on its own contragravity unit, spotlighted in orange to represent the KO sun, its two satellites circling about it as it revolved slowly.

"The globe itself is keeping perfect time, and Darius is all right. Xerxes is a few seconds of longitude ahead of true position."

"That's dreadful, Mr. Grego!" Stenson was deeply shocked. "I must adjust that the first thing tomorrow. I should have called to check on it long ago, but you know how it is. So many things to do, and so little time."

"I find the same trouble myself, Mr. Stenson."

They chatted for a while, and then Stenson apologized for taking up so much of Mr. Grego's valuable time. What he meant was that his own time, just as valuable to him, was wasting. After the screen blanked, Grego sat looking at it for a moment, wishing he had a hundred men like Henry Stenson in his own organization. Just men with Stenson's brains and character; wishing for a hundred instrument makers with Stenson's skills would have been unreasonable, even for wishing. There was only one Henry

Stenson, just as there had been only one Antonio Stradi-
vari. Why a man like that worked in a little shop on a
frontier planet like Zarathustra . . .

Then he looked, pridefully, at the globe. Alpha Continent had moved slowly to the right, with the little speck
that represented Mallorysport twinkling in the orange
light. Darius, the inner moon, where the Terra-Baldur-
Marduk Spacelines had their leased terminal, was almost
directly over it, and the outer moon, Xerxes, was edging
into sight. Xerxes was the one thing about Zarathustra
that the Company didn't own; the Terran Federation had
retained that as a naval base. It was the one reminder that
there was something bigger and more powerful than the
Company.

Gerd van Riebeek saw Ruth Ortheris leave the escalator, step aside and stand looking around the cocktail
lounge. He set his glass, with its inch of tepid highball, on
the bar; when her eyes shifted in his direction, he waved
to her, saw her brighten and wave back and then went to
meet her. She gave him a quick kiss on the cheek, dodged
when he reached for her and took his arm.

"Drink before we eat?" he asked.

"Oh, Lord, yes! I've just about had it for today."

He guided her toward one of the bartending machines,
inserted his credit key, and put a four-portion jug under
the spout, dialing the cocktail they always had when they
drank together. As he did, he noticed what she was wearing: short black jacket, lavender neckerchief, light gray
skirt. Not her usual vacation get-up.

"School department drag you back?" he asked as the
jug filled.

"Juvenile court." She got a couple of glasses from the
shelf under the machine as he picked up the jug. "A fif-
teen-year-old burglar."

They found a table at the rear of the room, out of the
worst of the cocktail-hour uproar. As soon as he filled her
glass, she drank half of it, then lit a cigarette.

"Junktown?" he asked.

She nodded. "Only twenty-five years since this planet
was discovered, and we have slums already. I was over
there most of the afternoon, with a pair of city police."

She didn't seem to want to talk about it. "What were you doing today?"

"Ruth, you ought to ask Doc Mallin to drop in on Leonard Kellogg sometime, and give him an unobstrusive going over."

"You haven't been having trouble with him again?" she asked anxiously.

He made a face, and then tasted his drink. "It's trouble just being around that character. Ruth, to use one of those expressions your profession deplores, Len Kellogg is just plain nuts!" He drank some more of his cocktail and helped himself to one of her cigarettes. "Here," he continued, after lighting it. "A couple of days ago, he told me he'd been getting inquiries about this plague of land-prawns they're having over on Beta. He wanted me to set up a research project to find out why and what to do about it."

"Well?"

"I did. I made two screen calls, and then I wrote a report and sent it up to him. That was where I jerked my trigger; I ought to have taken a couple of weeks and made a real production out of it."

"What did you tell him?"

"The facts. The limiting factor on land-prawn increase is the weather. The eggs hatch underground and the immature prawns dig their way out in the spring. If there's been a lot of rain, most of them drown in their holes or as soon as they emerge. According to growth rings on trees, last spring was the driest in the Beta Piedmont in centuries, so most of them survived, and as they're parthenogenetic females, they all laid eggs. This spring, it was even drier, so now they have land-prawns all over central Beta. And I don't know that anything can be done about them."

"Well, did he think you were just guessing?"

He shook his head in exasperation. "I don't know what he thinks. You're the psychologist, you try to figure it. I sent him that report yesterday morning. He seemed quite satisfied with it at the time. Today, just after noon, he sent for me and told me it wouldn't do at all. Tried to insist that the rainfall on Beta had been normal. That was silly; I referred him to his meteorologists and climatologists, where I'd gotten my information. He complained that the news services were after him for an explanation. I told him I'd given him the only explanation there was. He said he simply couldn't use it. There had to be some other explanation."

"If you don't like the facts, you ignore them, and if you need facts, dream up some you do like," she said. "That's typical rejection of reality. Not psychotic, not even psychoneurotic. But certainly not sane." She had finished her first drink and was sipping slowly at her second. "You know, this is interesting. Does he have some theory that would disqualify yours?"

"Not that I know of. I got the impression that he just didn't want the subject of rainfall on Beta discussed at all."

"That is odd. Has anything else peculiar been happening over on Beta lately?"

"No. Not that I know of," he repeated. "Of course, that swamp-drainage project over there was what caused the dry weather, last year and this year, but I don't see . . ." His own glass was empty, and when he tilted the jug over it, a few drops trickled out. He loooked at his watch. "Think we could have another cocktail before dinner?" he asked.

II

Jack Holloway landed the manipulator in front of the cluster of prefab huts. For a moment he sat still, realizing that he was tired, and then he climbed down from the control cabin and crossed the open grass to the door of the main living hut, opening it and reaching in to turn on the lights. Then he hesitated, looking up at Darius.

There was a wide ring around it, and he remembered noticing the wisps of cirrus clouds gathering overhead through the afternoon. Maybe it would rain tonight. This dry weather couldn't last forever. He'd been letting the manipulator stand out overnight lately. He decided to put it in the hangar. He went and opened the door of the vehicle shed, got back onto the machine and floated it inside. When he came back to the living hut, he saw that he had left the door wide open.

"Damn fool!" he rebuked himself. "Place could be crawling with prawns by now."

He looked quickly around the living room—under the big combination desk and library table, under the gunrack, under the chairs, back of the communication screen and the viewscreen, beyond the metal cabinet of the microfilm library—and saw nothing. Then he hung up his hat, took off his pistol and laid it on the table, and went back to the bathroom to wash his hands.

As soon as he put on the light, something inside the shower stall said, "*Yeeeek!*" in a startled voice.

He turned quickly, to see two wide eyes staring up at him out of a ball of golden fur. Whatever it was, it had a round head and big ears and a vaguely humanoid face with a little snub nose. It was sitting on its haunches, and in that position it was about a foot high. It had two tiny hands with opposing thumbs. He squatted to have a better look at it.

"Hello there, little fellow," he greeted it. "I never saw anything like you before. What are you anyhow?"

16

The small creature looked at him seriously and said, "Yeek," in a timid voice.

"Why, sure; you're a Little Fuzzy, that's what you are."

He moved closer, careful to make no alarmingly sudden movements, and kept on talking to it.

"Bet you slipped in while I left the door open. Well, if a Little Fuzzy finds a door open, I'd like to know why he shouldn't come in and look around."

He touched it gently. It started to draw back, then reached out a little hand and felt the material of his shirt-sleeve. He stroked it, and told it that it had the softest, silkiest fur ever. Then he took it on his lap. It yeeked in pleasure, and stretched an arm up around his neck.

"Why, sure; we're going to be good friends, aren't we? Would you like something to eat? Well, suppose you and I go see what we can find."

He put one hand under it, to support it like a baby—at least, he seemed to recall having seen babies supported in that way; babies were things he didn't fool with if he could help it—and straightened. It weighed between fifteen and twenty pounds. At first, it struggled in panic, then quieted and seemed to enjoy being carried. In the living room he sat down in his favorite armchair, under a standing lamp, and examined his new acquaintance.

It was a mammal—there was a fairly large mammalian class on Zarathustra—but beyond that he was stumped. It wasn't a primate, in the Terran sense. It wasn't like anything Terran, or anything else on Zarathustra. Being a biped put it in a class by itself for this planet. It was just a Little Fuzzy, and that was the best he could do.

That sort of nomenclature was the best anybody could do on a Class-III planet. On a Class-IV planet, say Loki, or Shesha, or Thor, naming animals was a cinch. You pointed to something and asked a native, and he'd gargle a mouthful of syllables at you, which might only mean, "Whaddaya wanna know for?" and you took it down in phonetic alphabet and the whatzit had a name. But on Zarathustra, there were no natives to ask. So this was a Little Fuzzy.

"What would you like to eat, Little Fuzzy?" he asked. "Open your mouth, and let Pappy Jack see what you have to chew with."

Little Fuzzy's dental equipment, allowing for the fact that his jaw was rounder, was very much like his own.

"You're probably omnivorous. How would you like some nice Terran Federation Space Forces Emergency Ration, Extraterrestrial, Type Three?" he asked.

Little Fuzzy made what sounded like an expression of willingness to try it. It would be safe enough; Extee Three had been fed to a number a Zarathustran mammals without ill effects. He carried Little Fuzzy out into the kitchen and put him on the floor, then got out a tin of the field ration and opened it, breaking off a small piece and handing it down. Little Fuzzy took the piece of golden-brown cake, sniffed at it, gave a delighted yeek and crammed the whole piece in his mouth.

"You never had to live on that stuff and nothing else for a month, that's for sure!"

He broke the cake in half and broke one half into manageable pieces and put it down on a saucer. Maybe Little Fuzzy would want a drink, too. He started to fill a pan with water, as he would for a dog, then looked at his visitor sitting on his haunches eating with both hands and changed his mind. He rinsed a plastic cup cap from an empty whisky bottle and put it down beside a deep bowl of water. Little Fuzzy was thirsty, and he didn't have to be shown what the cup was for.

It was too late to get himself anything elaborate; he found some leftovers in the refrigerator and combined them into a stew. While it was heating, he sat down at the kitchen table and lit his pipe. The spurt of flame from the lighter opened Little Fuzzy's eyes, but what really awed him was Pappy Jack blowing smoke. He sat watching this phenomenon, until, a few minutes later, the stew was hot and the pipe was laid aside; then Little Fuzzy went back to nibbling Extee Three.

Suddenly he gave a yeek of petulance and scampered into the living room. In a moment, he was back with something elongated and metallic which he laid on the floor beside him.

"What have you got there, Little Fuzzy? Let Pappy Jack see?"

Then he recognized it as his own one-inch wood chisel. He remembered leaving it in the outside shed after doing some work about a week ago, and not being able to find it when he had gone to look for it. That had worried him; people who got absent-minded about equipment didn't last long in the wilderness. After he finished eating and took the dishes to the sink, he went over and squatted beside his new friend.

"Let Pappy Jack look at it, Little Fuzzy," he said. "Oh, I'm not going to take it away from you. I just want to see it."

The edge was dulled and nicked; it had been used for a lot of things wood chisels oughtn't to be used for. Digging, and prying, and most likely, it had been used as a weapon. It was a handy-sized, all-purpose tool for a Little Fuzzy. He laid it on the floor where he had gotten it and started washing the dishes.

Little Fuzzy watched him with interest for a while, and then he began investigating the kitchen. Some of the things he wanted to investigate had to be taken away from him; at first that angered him, but he soon learned that there were things he wasn't supposed to have. Eventually, the dishes got washed.

There were more things to investigate in the living room. One of them was the wastebasket. He found that it could be dumped, and promptly dumped it, pulling out everything that hadn't fallen out. He bit a corner off a sheet of paper, chewed on it and spat it out in disgust. Then he found that crumpled paper could be flattened out and so he flatted a few sheets, and then discovered that it could also be folded. Then he got himself gleefully tangled in a snarl of wornout recording tape. Finally he lost interest and started away. Jack caught him and brought him back.

"No, Little Fuzzy," he said. "You do not dump wastebaskets and then walk away from them. You put things back in." He touched the container and said, slowly and distinctly, "Waste . . . basket." Then he righted it, doing it as Little Fuzzy would have to, and picked up a piece of paper, tossing it in from Little Fuzzy's shoulder height. Then he handed Little Fuzzy a wad of paper and repeated, "Waste . . . basket."

Little Fuzzy looked at him and said something that sounded as though it might be: "What's the matter with you, Pappy; you crazy or something?" After a couple more tries, however, he got it, and began throwing things in. In a few minutes, he had everything back in except a brightly colored plastic cartridge box and a wide-mouthed bottle with a screw cap. He held these up and said, "Yeek?"

"Yes, you can have them. Here; let Pappy Jack show you something."

He showed Little Fuzzy how the box could be opened and shut. Then, holding it where Little Fuzzy could watch, he unscrewed the cap and then screwed it on again.

"There, now. You try it."

Little Fuzzy looked up inquiringly, then took the bottle, sitting down and holding it between his knees. Unfortunately, he tried twisting it the wrong way and only screwed the cap on tighter. He yeeked plaintively.

"No, go ahead. You can do it."

Little Fuzzy look at the bottle again. Then he tried twisting the cap the other way, and it loosened. He gave a yeek that couldn't possibly be anything but "Eureka!" and promptly took it off, holding it up. After being commended, he examined both the bottle and the cap, feeling the threads, and then screwed the cap back on again.

"You know, you're a smart Little Fuzzy." It took a few seconds to realize just how smart. Little Fuzzy had wondered why you twisted the cap one way to take it off and the other way to put it on, and he had found out. For pure reasoning ability, that topped anything in the way of animal intelligence he'd ever seen. "I'm going to tell Ben Rainsford about you."

Going to the communication screen, he punched out the wave-length combination of the naturalist's camp, seventy miles down Snake River from the mouth of Cold Creek. Rainsford's screen must have been on automatic; it lit as soon as he was through punching. There was a card set up in front of it, lettered: AWAY ON TRIP, BACK THE FIFTEENTH. RECORDER ON.

"Ben, Jack Holloway," he said. "I just ran into something interesting." He explained briefly what it was. "I hope he stays around till you get back. He's totally unlike anything I've ever seen on this planet."

20

Little Fuzzy was disappointed when Jack turned off the screen; that had been interesting. He picked him up and carried him over to the armchair, taking him on his lap.

"Now," he said, reaching for the control panel of the viewscreen. "Watch this; we're going to see something nice."

When he put on the screen, at random, he got a view, from close up, of the great fires that were raging where the Company people were burning off the dead forests on what used to be Big Blackwater Swamp. Little Fuzzy cried out in alarm, flung his arms around Pappy Jack's neck and buried his face in the bosom of his shirt. Well, forest fires started from lightning sometimes, and they'd be bad things for a Little Fuzzy. He worked the selector and got another pickup, this time on the top of Company House in Mallorysport, three time zones west, with the city spread out below and the sunset blazing in the west. Little Fuzzy stared at it in wonder. It was pretty impressive for a little fellow who'd spent all his life in the big woods.

So was the spaceport, and a lot of other things he saw, though a view of the planet as a whole from Darius puzzled him considerably. Then, in the middle of a symphony orchestra concert from Mallorysport Opera House, he wriggled loose, dropped to the floor and caught up his wood chisel, swinging it back over his shoulder like a two-handed sword.

"What the devil? Oh-oh!"

A land-prawn, which must have gotten in while the door was open, was crossing the living room. Little Fuzzy ran after and past it, pivoted and brought the corner of the chisel edge down on the prawn's neck, neatly beheading it. He looked at his victim for a moment, then slid the chisel under it and flopped it over on its back, slapping it twice with the flat and cracking the undershell. Then he began pulling the dead prawn apart, tearing out pieces of meat and eating them delicately. After disposing of the larger chunks, he used the chisel to chop off one of the prawn's mandibles to use as a pick to get at the less accessible morsels. When he had finished, he licked his fingers clean and started back to the armchair.

"No." Jack pointed at the prawn shell. "Wastebasket."

"Yeek?"

"Wastebasket."

Little Fuzzy gathered up the bits of shell, putting them where they belonged. Then he came back and climbed up on Pappy Jack's lap, and looked at things in the screen until he fell asleep.

Jack lifted him carefully and put him down on the warm chair seat without wakening him, then went to the kitchen, poured himself a drink and brought it in to the big table, where he lit his pipe and began writing up his diary for the day. After a while, Little Fuzzy woke, found that the lap he had gone to sleep on had vanished, and yeeked disconsolately.

A folded blanket in one corner of the bedroom made a satisfactory bed, once Little Fuzzy had assured himself that there were no bugs in it. He brought in his bottle and his plastic box and put them on the floor beside it. Then he ran to the front door in the living room and yeeked to be let out. Going about twenty feet from the house, he used the chisel to dig a small hole, and after it had served its purpose he filled it in carefully and came running back.

Well, maybe Fuzzies were naturally gregarious, and were homemakers—den-holes, or nests, or something like that. Nobody wants messes made in the house, and when the young ones did it, their parents would bang them around to teach them better manners. This was Little Fuzzy's home now; he knew how he ought to behave in it.

The next morning at daylight, he was up on the bed, trying to dig Pappy Jack out from under the blankets. Besides being a most efficient land-prawn eradicator, he made a first rate alarm clock. But best of all, he was Pappy Jack's Little Fuzzy. He wanted out; this time Jack took his movie camera and got the whole operation on film. One thing, there'd have to be a little door, with a spring to hold it shut, that Little Fuzzy could operate himself. That was designed during breakfast. It only took a couple of hours to make and install it; Little Fuzzy got the idea as soon as he saw it, and figured out how to work it for himself.

Jack went back to the workshop, built a fire on the hand forge and forged a pointed and rather broad blade, four inches long, on the end of a foot of quarter-inch round tool-steel. It was too point-heavy when finished, so he welded a knob on the other end to balance it. Little Fuzzy knew what that was for right away; running outside, he dug a couple of practice holes with it, and then began casting about in the grass for land-prawns.

Jack followed him with the camera and got movies of a couple of prawn killings, accomplished with smooth, by-the-numbers precision. Little Fuzzy hadn't learned that chop-slap-slap routine in the week since he had found the wood chisel.

Going into the shed, he hunted for something without more than a general idea of what it would look like, and found it where Little Fuzzy had discarded it when he found the chisel. It was a stock of hardwood a foot long, rubbed down and polished smooth, apparently with sandstone. There was a paddle at one end, with enough of an edge to behead a prawn, and the other end had been worked to a point. He took it into the living hut and sat down at the desk to examine it with a magnifying glass. Bits of soil embedded in the sharp end—that had been used as a pick. The paddle end had been used as a shovel, beheader and shell-cracker. Little Fuzzy had known exactly what he wanted when he'd started making that thing, he'd kept on until it was as perfect as possible, and had stopped short of spoiling it by overrefinement.

Finally, Jack put it away in the top drawer of the desk. He was thinking about what to get for lunch when Little Fuzzy burst into the living room, clutching his new weapon and yeeking excitedly.

"What's the matter, kid? You got troubles?" He rose and went to the gunrack, picking down a rifle and checking the chamber. "Show Pappy Jack what it is."

Little Fuzzy followed him to the big door for human-type people, ready to bolt back inside if necessary. The trouble was a harpy—a thing about the size and general design of a Terran Jurassic pterodactyl, big enough to take a Little Fuzzy at one mouthful. It must have made one swoop at him already, and was circling back for another. It ran into a 6-mm rifle bullet, went into a backward loop and dropped like a stone.

Little Fuzzy made a very surprised remark, looked at the dead harpy for a moment and then spotted the ejected empty cartridge. He grabbed it and held it up, asking if he could have it. When told that he could, he ran back to the bedroom with it. When he returned, Pappy Jack picked him up and carried him to the hangar and up into the control cabin of the manipulator.

The throbbing of the contragravity-field generator and the sense of rising worried him at first, but after they had picked up the harpy with the grapples and risen to five hundred feet he began to enjoy the ride. They dropped the harpy a couple of miles up what the latest maps were designating as Holloway's Run, and then made a wide circle back over the mountains. Little Fuzzy thought it was fun.

After lunch, Little Fuzzy had a nap on Pappy Jack's bed. Jack took the manipulator up to the diggings, put off a couple more shots, uncovered more flint and found another sunstone. It wasn't often that he found stones on two successive days. When he returned to the camp, Little Fuzzy was picking another land-prawn apart in front of the living hut.

After dinner—Little Fuzzy liked cooked food, too, if it wasn't too hot—they went into the living room. He remembered having seen a bolt and nut in the desk drawer when he had been putting the wooden prawn-killer away, and he got it out, showing it to Little Fuzzy. Little Fuzzy studied it for a moment, then ran into the bedroom and came back with his screw-top bottle. He took the top off, put it on again and then screwed the nut off the bolt, holding it up.

"See, Pappy?" Or yeeks to that effect. "Nothing to it."

Then he unscrewed the bottle top, dropped the bolt inside after replacing the nut and screwed the cap on again.

"Yeek," he said, with considerable self-satisfaction.

He had a right to be satisfied with himself. What he'd been doing had been generalizing. Bottle tops and nuts belonged to the general class of things-that-screwed-onto-things. To take them off, you turned left; to put them on again, you turned right, after making sure that the threads engaged. And since he could conceive of right- and left-handedness, that might mean that he could think of properties apart from objects, and that was forming abstract ideas. Maybe that was going a little far, but . . .

24

"You know, Pappy Jack's got himself a mighty smart Little Fuzzy. Are you a grown-up Little Fuzzy, or are you just a baby Litttle Fuzzy? Shucks, I'll bet you're Professor Doctor Fuzzy."

He wondered what to give the professor, if that was what he was, to work on next, and he doubted the wisdom of teaching him too much about taking things apart, just at present. Sometime he might come home and find something important taken apart, or, worse, taken apart and put together incorrectly. Finally, he went to a closet, rummaging in it until he found a tin cannister. By the time he returned, Little Fuzzy had gotten up on the chair, found his pipe in the ashtray and was puffing on it and coughing.

"Hey, I don't think that's good for you!"

He recovered the pipe, wiped the stem on his shirt-sleeve and put it in his mouth, then placed the cannister on the floor, and put Little Fuzzy on the floor beside it. There were about ten pounds of stones in it. When he had first settled here, he had made a collection of the local minerals, and, after learning what he'd wanted to, he had thrown them out, all but twenty or thirty of the prettiest specimens. He was glad, now, that he had kept these.

Little Fuzzy looked the can over, decided that the lid was a member of the class of things-that-screwed-onto-things and got it off. The inside of the lid was mirror-shiny, and it took him a little thought to discover that what he saw in it was only himself. He yeeked about that, and looked into the can. This, he decided, belonged to the class of things-that-can-be-dumped, like wastebaskets, so he dumped it on the floor. Then he began examining the stones and sorting them by color.

Except for an interest in colorful views on the screen, this was the first real evidence that Fuzzies possessed color perception. He proceeded to give further and more impressive proof, laying out the stones by shade, in correct spectral order, from a lump of amethystlike quartz to a dark red stone. Well, maybe he'd seen rainbows. Maybe he'd lived near a big misty waterfall, where there was always a rainbow when the sun was shining. Or maybe that was just his natural way of seeing colors.

Then, when he saw what he had to work with, he began

25

making arrangements with them, laying them out in odd circular and spiral patterns. Each time he finished a pattern, he would yeek happily to call attention to it, sit and look at it for a while, and then take it apart and start a new one. Little Fuzzy was capable of artistic gratification too. He made useless things, just for the pleasure of making and looking at them.

Finally, he put the stones back into the tin, put the lid on and rolled it into the bedroom, righting it beside his bed along with his other treasures. The new weapon he laid on the blanket beside him when he went to bed.

The next morning, Jack broke up a whole cake of Extee Three and put it down, filled the bowl with water, and, after making sure he had left nothing lying around that Little Fuzzy could damage or on which he might hurt himself, took the manipulator up to the diggings. He worked all morning, cracking nearly a ton and a half of flint, and found nothing. Then he set off a string of shots, brought down an avalanche of sandstone and exposed more flint, and sat down under a pool-ball tree to eat his lunch.

Half an hour after he went back to work, he found the fossil of some jellyfish that hadn't eaten the right things in the right combinations, but a little later, he found four nodules, one after another, and two of them were sunstones; four or five chunks later, he found a third. Why, this must be the Dying Place of the Jellyfish! By late afternoon, when he had cleaned up all his loose flint, he had nine, including one deep red monster an inch in diameter. There must have been some connection current in the ancient ocean that had swirled them all into this one place. He considered setting off some more shots, decided that it was too late and returned to camp.

"Little Fuzzy!" he called, opening the living-room door. "Where are you, Little Fuzzy? Pappy Jack's rich; we're going to celebrate!"

Silence. He called again; still no reply or scamper of feet. Probably cleaned up all the prawns around the camp and went hunting farther out into the woods, thought Jack. Unbuckling his gun and dropping it onto the table, he went out to the kitchen. Most of the Extee Three was gone. In the bedroom, he found that Little Fuzzy had dumped the stones out of the biscuit tin and made an arrangement, and laid the wood chisel in a neat diagonal across the blanket.

After getting dinner assembled and in the oven, he went out and called for a while, then mixed a highball and took it into the living room, sitting down with it to go over his day's findings. Rather incredulously, he realized that he had cracked out at least seventy-five thousand sols' worth of stones today. He put them into the bag and sat sipping the highball and thinking pleasant thoughts until the bell on the stove warned him that dinner was ready.

He ate alone—after all the years he had been doing that contentedly, it had suddenly become intolerable—and in the evening he dialed through his microfilm library, finding only books he had read and re-read a dozen times, or books he kept for reference. Several times he thought he heard the little door open, but each time he was mistaken. Finally he went to bed.

As soon as he woke, he looked across at the folded blanket, but the wood chisel was still lying athwart it. He put down more Extee Three and changed the water in the bowl before leaving for the diggings. That day he found three more sunstones, and put them in the bag mechanically and without pleasure. He quit work early and spent over an hour spiraling around the camp, but saw nothing. The Extee Three in the kitchen was untouched.

Maybe the little fellow ran into something too big for him, even with his fine new weapon—a hobthrush, or a bush-goblin, or another harpy. Or maybe he'd just gotten tired staying in one place, and had moved on.

No; he'd liked it here. He'd had fun, and been happy. He shook his head sadly. Once he, too, had lived in a pleasant place, where he'd had fun, and could have been happy if he hadn't thought there was something he'd had to do. So he had gone away, leaving grieved people behind him. Maybe that was how it was with Little Fuzzy. Maybe he didn't realize how much of a place he had made for himself here, or how empty he was leaving it.

He started for the kitchen to get a drink, and checked himself. Take a drink because you pity yourself, and then the drink pities you and has a drink, and then two good

27

drinks get together and that calls for drinks all around. No; he'd have one drink, maybe a little bigger than usual, before he went to bed.

III

He started awake, rubbed his eyes and looked at the clock. Past twenty-two hundred; now it really was time for a drink, and then to bed. He rose stiffly and went out to the kitchen, pouring the whisky and bringing it in to the table desk, where he sat down and got out his diary. He was almost finished with the day's entry when the little door behind him opened and a small voice said, "Yeeek." He turned quickly.

"Little Fuzzy?"

The small sound was repeated, impatiently. Little Fuzzy was holding the door open, and there was an answer from outside. Then another Fuzzy came in, and another; four of them, one carrying a tiny, squirming ball of white fur in her arms. They all had prawn-killers like the one in the drawer, and they stopped just inside the room and gaped about them in bewilderment. Then, laying down his weapon, Little Fuzzy ran to him; stooping from the chair, he caught him and then sat down on the floor with him.

"So that's why you ran off and worried Pappy Jack? You wanted your family here, too!"

The others piled the things they were carrying with Little Fuzzy's steel weapon and approached hesitantly. He talked to them, and so did Little Fuzzy—at least it sounded like that—and finally one came over and fingered his shirt, and then reached up and pulled his mustache. Soon all of them were climbing onto him, even the female with the baby. It was small enough to sit on his palm, but in a minute it had climbed to his shoulder, and then it was sitting on his head.

"You people want dinner?" he asked.

Little Fuzzzy yeeked emphatically; that was a word he recognized. He took them all into the kitchen and tried them on cold roast veldbeest and yummiyams and fried pool-ball fruit; while they were eating from a couple of big pans, he went back to the living room to examine the

29

things they had brought with them. Two of the prawn-killers were wood, like the one Little Fuzzy had discarded in the shed. A third was of horn, beautifully polished, and the fourth looked as though it had been made from the shoulder bone of something like a zebralope. Then there was a small *coup de poing* ax, rather low paleolithic, and a chipped implement of flint the shape of a slice of orange and about five inches along the straight edge. For a hand the size of his own, he would have called it a scraper. He puzzled over it for a while, noticed that the edge was serrated, and decided that it was a saw. And there were three very good flake knives, and some shells, evidently drinking vessels.

Mamma Fuzzy came in while he was finishing the examination. She seemed suspicious, until she saw that none of the family property had been taken or damaged. Baby Fuzzy was clinging to her fur with one hand and holding a slice of pool-ball fruit, on which he was munching, with the other. He crammed what was left of the fruit into his mouth, climbed up on Jack and sat down on his head again. Have to do something to break him of that. One of these days, he'd be getting too big for it.

In a few minutes, the rest of the family came in, chasing and pummeling each other and yeeking happily. Mama jumped off his lap and joined the free-for-all, and then Baby took off from his head and landed on Mama's back. And he thought he'd lost his Little Fuzzy, and, gosh, here he had five Fuzzies and a Baby Fuzzy. When they were tired romping, he made beds for them in the living room, and brought out Little Fuzzy's bedding and his treasures. One Little Fuzzy in the bedroom was just fine; five and a Baby Fuzzy were a little too much of a good thing.

They were swarming over the bed, Baby and all, to waken him the next morning.

The next morning he made a steel chopper-digger for each of them, and half a dozen extras for replacements in case more Fuzzies showed up. He also made a miniature ax with a hardwood handle, a handsaw out of a piece of broken power-saw blade and half a dozen little knives forged in one piece from quarter-inch coil-spring material. He had less trouble trading the Fuzzies' own things away from them than he had expected. They had a very keen property sense, but they knew a good deal when one was offered. He put the wooden and horn and bone and stone artifacts away in the desk drawer. Start of the Holloway Collection of Zarathustran Fuzzy Weapons and Implements. Maybe he'd will it to the Federation Institute of Zeno-Sciences.

Of course, the family had to try out the new chopper-diggers on land-prawns, and he followed them around with the movie camera. They killed a dozen and a half that morning, and there was very little interest in lunch, though they did sit around nibbling, just to be doing what he was doing. As soon as they finished, they all went in for a nap on his bed. He spent the afternoon pottering about camp doing odd jobs that he had been postponing for months. The Fuzzies all emerged in the late afternoon for a romp in the grass outside.

He was in the kitchen, getting dinner, when they all came pelting in through the little door into the living room, making an excited outcry. Little Fuzzy and one of the other males came into the kitchen. Little Fuzzzy squatted, put one hand on his lower jaw, with thumb and little finger extended, and the other on his forehead, first finger upright. Then he thrust out his right arm stiffly and made a barking noise of a sort he had never made before. He had to do it a second time before Jack got it.

There was a large and unpleasant carnivore, called a damnthing—another example of zoological nomenclature on uninhabited planets—which had a single horn on its forehead and one on either side of the lower jaw. It was something for Fuzzies, and even for human-type people, to get excited about. He laid down the paring knife and the yummiyam he had been peeling, wiped his hands and went into the living room, taking a quick nose count and satisfying himself that none of the family were missing as he crossed to the gunrack.

This time, instead of the 6-mm he had used on the harpy, he lifted down the big 12.7 double express, making sure that it was loaded and pocketing a few spare rounds. Little Fuzzy followed him outside, pointing around the living hut to the left. The rest of the family stayed indoors.

Stepping out about twenty feet, he started around

counter-clockwise. There was no damnthing on the north side, and he was about to go around to the east side when Little Fuzzy came dashing past him, pointing to the rear. He whirled, to see the damnthing charging him from behind, head down, and middle horn lowered. He should have thought of that; damnthings would double and hunt their hunters.

He lined the sights instinctively and squeezed. The big rifle roared and banged his shoulder, and the bullet caught the damnthing and hurled all half-ton of it backward. The second shot caught it just below one of the fungoid-looking ears, and the beast gave a spasmotic all-over twitch and was still. He reloaded mechanically, but there was no need for a third shot. The damnthing was as dead as he would have been except for Little Fuzzy's warning.

He mentioned that to Little Fuzzy, who was calmly retrieving the empty cartridges. Then, rubbing his shoulder where the big rifle had pounded him, he went in and returned the weapon to the rack. He used the manipulator to carry the damnthing away from the camp and drop it into a treetop, where it would furnish a welcome if puzzling treat for the harpies.

There was another alarm in the evening after dinner. The family had come in from their sunset romp and were gathered in the living room, where Little Fuzzy was demonstrating the principle of things-that-screwed-onto-things with the wide-mouthed bottle and the bolt and nut, when something huge began hooting directly overhead. They all froze, looking up at the ceiling, and then ran over and got under the gunrack. This must be something far more serious than a damnthing, and what Pappy Jack would do about it would be nothing short of catastrophic. They were startled to see Pappy Jack merely go to the door, open it and step outside. After all, none of them had ever heard a Constabulary aircar klaxon before.

The car settled onto the grass in front of the camp, gave a slight lurch and went off contragravity. Two men in uniform got out, and in the moonlight he recognized both of them: Lieutenant George Lunt and his driver, Ahmed Khadra. He called a greeting to them.

"Anything wrong?" he asked.

"No; just thought we'd drop in and see how you were making out," Lunt told him. "We don't get up this way often. Haven't had any trouble lately, have you?"

"Not since the last time." The last time had been a couple of woods tramps, out-of-work veldbeest herders from the south, who had heard about the little bag he carried around his neck. All the Constabulary had needed to do was remove the bodies and write up a report. "Come on in and hang up your guns awhile. I have something I want to show you."

Little Fuzzy had come out and was pulling at his trouser leg; he stooped and picked him up, setting him on his shoulder. The rest of the family, deciding that it must be safe, had come to the door and were looking out.

"Hey! What the devil are those things?" Lunt asked, stopping short halfway from the car.

"Fuzzies. Mean to tell me you've never seen Fuzzies before?"

"No, I haven't. What are they?"

The two Constabulary men came closer, and Jack stepped back into the house, shooing the Fuzzies out of the way. Lunt and Khadra stopped inside the door.

"I just told you. They're Fuzzies. That's all the name I know for them."

A couple of Fuzzies came over and looked up at Lieutenant Lunt; one of them said, "Yeek?"

"They want to know what you are, so that makes it mutual."

Lunt hesitated for a moment, then took off his belt and holster and hung it on one of the pegs inside the door, putting his beret over it. Khadra followed his example promptly. That meant that they considered themselves temporarily off duty and would accept a drink if one were offered. A Fuzzy was pulling at Ahmed Khadra's trouser leg and asking to be noticed, and Mamma Fuzzy was holding Baby up to show to Lunt. Khadra, rather hesitantly, picked up the Fuzzy who was trying to attract his ʌntion.

ʌaw anything like them before, Jack," he said.

things."

"They won't hurt me, Lieutenant; they haven't hurt Jack, have they?" He sat down on he floor, and a couple more came to him. "Why don't you get acquainted with them? They're cute."

George Lunt wouldn't let one of his men do anything he was afraid to do; he sat down on the floor, too, and Mamma brought her baby to him. Immediately, the baby jumped onto his shoulder and tried to get onto his head.

"Relax, George," Jack told him. "They're just Fuzzies; they want to make friends with you."

"I'm always worried about strange life forms," Lunt said. "You've been around enough to know some of the things that have happened—"

"They are not a strange life form; they are Zarathus-tran mammals. The same life form you've had for dinner every day since you came here. Their biochemistry's identical with ours. Think they'll give you the Polka-Dot Plague, or something?" He put Little Fuzzy down on the floor with the others. "We've been exploring this planet for twenty-five years, and nobody's found anything like that here."

"You said it yourself, Lieutenant," Khadra put in. "Jack's been around enough to know."

"Well . . . They are cute little fellows." Lunt lifted Baby down off his head and gave him back to Mamma. Little Fuzzy had gotten hold of the chain of his whistle and was trying to find out what was on the other end. "Bet they're a lot of company for you."

"You just get acquainted with them. Make yourselves at home; I'll go rustle up some refreshments."

While he was in the kitchen, filling a soda siphon and getting ice out of the refrigerator, a police whistle began shrilling in the living room. He was opening a bottle of whisky when Little Fuzzy came dashing out, blowing on it, a couple more of the family pursuing him and trying to get it away from him. He opened a tin of Extee Three for the Fuzzies; as he did, another whistle in the living room began blowing.

"We have a whole shoebox full of them at th___" Lunt yelled to him above the din. "_____ two off as ex_____" that the Fuzzies appreciate that. Ahmed, suppose you do the bartending while I give the kids their candy."

By the time Khadra had the drinks mixed and he had distributed the Extee Three to the Fuzzies, Lunt had gotten into the easy chair, and the Fuzzies were sitting on the floor in front of him, still looking him over curiously. At least the Extee Three had taken their minds off the whistles for a while.

"What I want to know, Jack, is where they came from," Lunt said, taking his drink. "I've been up here for five years, and I never saw anything like them before."

"I've been here five years longer, and I never saw them before, either. I think they came down from the north, from the country between the Cordilleras and the West Coast Range. Outside of an air survey at ten thousand feet and a few spot landings here and there, none of that country has been explored. For all anybody knows, it could be full of Fuzzies."

He began with his first encounter with Little Fuzzy, and by the time he had gotten as far as the wood chisel and the killing of the land-prawn, Lunt and Khadra were looking at each other in amazement.

"That's it!" Khadra said. "I've found prawn-shells cracked open and the meat picked out, just the way you describe it. I always wondered what did that. But they don't all have wood chisels. What do you suppose they used ordinarily?"

"Ah!" He pulled the drawer open and began getting things out. "Here's the one Little Fuzzy discarded when he found my chisel. The rest of this stuff the others brought in when they came."

Lunt and Khadra rose and came over to look at the things. Lunt tried to argue that the Fuzzies couldn't have made that stuff. He wasn't even able to convince himself. Having finished their Extee Three, the Fuzzies were looking expectantly at the viewscreen, and it occurrred to him that none of them except Little Fuzzy had ever seen it on. Then Little Fuzzy jumped up on the chair Lunt had vacated, reached over to the control-panel and switched it on. What he got was an empty stretch of moonlit plain to the south, from a pickup on one of the steel towers the veldbeest herders used. That wasn't very interesting; he twiddled the selector and finally got a night soccer game at Mallorysport. That was just fine; he jumped down and joined the others in front of the screen.

"I've seen Terran monkeys and Freyan Kholphs that liked to watch screens and could turn them on and work the selector," Lunt said. It sounded like the token last salvo before the surrender.

"Kholphs are smart," Khadra agreed. "They use tools."

"Do they make tools? Or tools to make tools with, like that saw?" There was no argument on that. "No. Nobody does that except people like us and the Fuzzies.

It was the first time he had come right out and said that; the first time he had even consciously thought it. He realized that he had been convinced of it all along, though. It startled the constabulary lieutenant and trooper.

"You mean you think—?" Lunt began.

"They don't talk, and they don't build fires," Ahmed Khadra said, as though that settled it.

"Ahmed, you know better than that. That talk-and-build-a-fire rule isn't any scientific test at all."

"It's a legal test." Lunt supported his subordinate.

"It's a rule-of-thumb that was set up so that settlers on new planets couldn't get away with murdering and enslaving the natives by claiming they thought they were only hunting and domesticating wild animals," he said. "Anything that talks and builds a fire is a sapient being, yes. That's the law. But that doesn't mean that anything that doesn't isn't. I haven't seen any of this gang building fires, and as I don't want to come home sometime and find myself burned out, I'm not going to teach them. But I'm sure they have some means of communication among themselves."

"Has Ben Rainsford seen them yet?" Lunt asked.

"Ben's off on a trip somewhere. I called him as soon as Little Fuzzy, over there, showed up here. He won't be back till Friday."

"Yes, that's right; I did know that." Lunt was still looking dubiously at the Fuzzies. "I'd like to hear what he thinks about them."

If Ben said they were safe, Lunt would accept that. Ben was an expert, and Lunt respected expert testimony. Until

36

then, he wasn't sure. He'd probably order a medical check-up for himself and Khadra the first thing tomorrow, to make sure they hadn't picked up some kind of bug.

IV

The Fuzzies took the manipulator quite calmly the next morning. That wasn't any horrible monster, that was just something Pappy Jack took rides in. He found one rather indifferent sunstone in the morning and two good ones in the afternoon. He came home early and found the family in the living room; they had dumped the wastebasket and were putting things back into it. Another land-prawn seemed to have gotten into the house; its picked shell was with the other rubbish in the basket. They had dinner early, and he loaded the lot of them into the airjeep and took them for a long ride to the south and west.

The following day, he located the flint vein on the other side of the gorge and spent most of the morning blasting away the sandstone above it. The next time he went into Mallorysport, he decided, he was going to shop around for a good power-shovel. He had to blast a channel to keep the little stream from damming up on him. He didn't get any flint cracked at all that day. There was another harpy circling around the camp when he got back; he chased it with the manipulator and shot it down with his pistol. Harpies probably found Fuzzies as tasty as Fuzzies found land-prawns. The family were all sitting under the gunrack when he entered the living room.

The next day he cracked flint, and found three more stones. It really looked as though he had found the Dying Place of the Jellyfish at that. He knocked off early that afternoon, and when he came in sight of the camp, he saw an airjeep grounded on the lawn and a small man with a red beard in a faded Khaki bush-jacket sitting on the bench by the kitchen door, surrounded by Fuzzies. There was a camera and some other equipment laid up where the Fuzzies couldn't get at it. Baby Fuzzy, of course, was sitting on his head. He looked up and waved, and then handed Baby to his mother and rose to his feet.

38

"Well, what do you think of them, Ben?" Jack called down, as he grounded the manipulator.

"My God, don't start me on that now!" Ben Rainsford replied, and then laughed. "I stopped at the constabulary post on the way home. I thought George Lunt had turned into the biggest liar in the known galaxy. Then I went home, and found your call on the recorder, so I came over here."

"Been waiting long?"

The Fuzzies had all abandoned Rainsford and come trooping over as soon as the manipulator was off contragravity. He climbed down among them, and they followed him across the grass, catching at his trouser legs and yeeking happily.

"Not so long." Rainsford looked at his watch. "Good Lord, three and a half hours is all. Well, the time passed quickly. You know, your little fellows have good ears. They heard you coming a long time before I did."

"Did you see them killing any prawns?"

"I should say! I got a lot of movies of it." He shook his head slowly. "Jack, this is almost incredible."

"You're staying for dinner, of course?"

"You try and chase me away. I want to hear all about this. Want you to make a tape about them, if you're willing."

"Glad to. We'll do that after we eat." He sat down on the bench, and the Fuzzies began climbing upon and beside him. "This is the original, Little Fuzzy. He brought the rest in a couple of days later. Mamma Fuzzy, and Baby Fuzzy. And these are Mike and Mitzi. I call this one Ko-Ko, because of the ceremonious way he beheads landprawns."

"George says you call them all Fuzzies. Want that for the official designation?"

"Sure. That's what they are, isn't it?"

"Well, let's call the order Hollowayans," Rainsford said. "Family, Fuzzies; genus, Fuzzy. Species, Holloway's Fuzzy —*Fuzzy fuzzy holloway*. How'll that be?"

That would be all right, he supposed. At least, they didn't try to Latinize things in extraterrestrial zoology any more.

"I supppose our bumper crop of land-prawns is what brought them into this section?"

"Yes, of course. George was telling me you thought they'd come down from the north; about the only place they could have come from. This is probably just the advance guard; we'll be having Fuzzies all over the place before long. I wonder how fast they breed."

"Not very fast. Three males and two females in this crowd, and only one young one." He set Mike and Mitzi off his lap and got to his feet. "I'll go start dinner now. While I'm doing that, you can look at the stuff they brought in with them."

When he had placed the dinner in the oven and taken a couple of highballs into the living room, Rainsford was still sitting at the desk, looking at the artifacts. He accepted his drink and sipped it absently, then raised his head.

"Jack, this stuff is absolutely amazing," he said.

"It's better than that. It's unique. Only collection of native weapons and implements on Zarathustra."

Ben Rainsford looked up sharply. "You mean what I think you mean?" he asked. "Yes; you do." He drank some of his highball, set down the glass and picked up the polished-horn prawn-killer. "Anything—pardon, anybody —who does this kind of work is good enough native for me." He hesitated briefly. "Why, Jack this tape you said you'd make. Can I transmit a copy to Juan Jimenez? He's chief mammalogist with the Company science division; we exchange information. And there's another Company man I'd like to have hear it. Gerd van Riebeek. He's a general xeno-naturalist, like me, but he's especially interested in animal evolution."

"Why not? The Fuzzies are a scientific discovery. Discoveries ought to be reported."

Little Fuzzy, Mike and Mitzi strolled in from the kitchen. Little Fuzzy jumped up on the armchair and switched on the viewscreen. Fiddling with the selector, he got the Big Blackwater woods-burning. Mike and Mitzi shrieked delightedly, like a couple of kids watching a horror show. They knew, by now, that nothing in the screen could get out and hurt them.

"Would you mind if they came out here and saw the Fuzzies?"

"Why, the Fuzzies would love that. They like company."

Mamma and Baby and Ko-Ko came in, seemed to approve what was on the screen and sat down to watch it. When the bell on the stove rang, they all got up, and Ko-Ko jumped onto the chair and snapped the screen off. Ben Rainsford looked at him for a moment.

"You know, I have married friends with children who have a hell of a time teaching eight-year-olds to turn off screens when they're through watching them," he commented.

It took an hour, after dinner, to get the whole story, from the first little yeek in the shower stall, on tape. When he had finished, Ben Rainsford made a few remarks and shut off the recorder, then looked at his watch.

"Twenty hundred; it'll be seventeen hundred in Mallorysport," he said. "It could catch Jimenez at Science Center if I called now. He usually works a little late."

"Go ahead. Want to show him some Fuzzies?" He moved his pistol and some other impedimenta off the table and set Little Fuzzy and Mamma Fuzzy and Baby upon it, then drew up a chair beside it, in range of the communication screen, and sat down with Mike and Mitzi and Ko-Ko. Rainsford punched out a wave-length combination. Then he picked up Baby Fuzzy and set him on his head.

In a moment, the screen flickered and cleared, and a young man looked out of it, with the momentary upward glance of one who wants to make sure his public face is on straight. It was a bland, tranquilized, life-adjusted, group-integrated sort of face—the face turned out in thousands of copies every year by the educational production lines on Terra.

"Why, Bennett, this is a pleasant surprise," he began. "I never expec—" Then he choked; at least, he emitted a sound of surprise. "What in the name of Dai-Butsu are those things on the table in front of you?" he demanded. "I never saw anything—*And what is that on your head?*"

"Family group of Fuzzies," Rainsford said. "Mature male, mature female, immature male." He lifted Baby Fuzzy down and put him in Mamma's arms. Species *Fuzzy*

41

fuzzy holloway zarathustra. The gentleman on my left is Jack Holloway, the sunstone operator, who is the original discoverer. Jack, Juan Jimenez."

They shook their own hands at one another in the ancient Terran-Chinese gesture that was used on communication screens, and assured each other—Jimenez rather absently—that it was a pleasure. He couldn't take his eyes off the Fuzzies.

"Where did they come from?" he wanted to know. "Are you sure they're indigenous?"

"They're not quite up to spaceships, yet, Dr. Jimenez. Fairly early Paleolithic, I'd say."

Jimenez thought he was joking, and laughed. The sort of a laugh that could be turned on and off, like a light. Rainsford assured him that the Fuzzies were really indigenous.

"We have everything that's known about them on tape," he said. "About an hour of it. Can you take sixty-speed?" He was making adjustments on the recorder as he spoke. "All right, set and we'll transmit to you. And can you get hold of Gerd van Riebeek? I'd like him to hear it too; it's as much up his alley as anybody's."

When Jimenez was ready, Rainsford pressed the play-off button, and for a minute the recorder gave a high, wavering squeak. The Fuzzies all looked startled. Then it ended.

"I think, when you hear this, that you and Gerd will both want to come out and see these little people. If you can, bring somebody who's a qualified psychologist, somebody capable of evaluating the Fuzzies' mentation. Jack wasn't kidding about early Paleolithic. If they're not sapient, they only miss it by about one atomic diameter."

Jimenez looked almost as startled as the Fuzzies had. "You surely don't mean that?" He looked from Rainsford to Jack Holloway and back. "Well, I'll call you back, when we've both heard the tape. You're three time zones west of us, aren't you? Then we'll try to make it before your midnight—that'll be twenty-one hundred."

He called back half an hour short of that. This time, it was from the living room of an apartment instead of an office. There was a portable record player in the foreground and a low table with snacks and drinks, and two other people were with him. One was a man of about Jimenez's age with a good-humored, non-life-adjusted, non-group-integrated and slightly weather-beaten face. The other was a woman with glossy black hair and a Mona Lisa-ish smile. The Fuzzies had gotten sleepy, and had been bribed with Extee Three to stay up a little longer. Immediately, they registered interest. This was more fun than the viewscreen.

Jimenez introduced his companions as Gerd van Riebeek and Ruth Ortheris. "Ruth is with Dr. Mallin's section; she's been working with the school department and the juvenile court. She can probably do as well with your Fuzzies as a regular xeno-psychologist."

"Well, I have worked with extraterrestrials," the woman said. "I've been on Loki and Thor and Shesha."

Jack nodded. "Been on the same planets myself. Are you people coming out here?"

"Oh, yes," van Riebeek said. "We'll be out by noon tomorrow. We may stay a couple of days, but that won't put you to any trouble; I have a boat that's big enough for the three of us to camp on. Now, how do we get to your place?"

Jack told him, and gave map coordinates. Van Riebeek noted them down.

"'There's one thing, though, I'm going to have to get firm about. I don't want to have to speak about it again. These little people are to be treated with consideration, and not as laboratory animals. You will not hurt them, or annoy them, or force them to do anything they don't want to do."

"We understand that. We won't do anything with the Fuzzies without your approval. Is there anything you'd want us to bring out?"

"Yes. A few things for the camp that I'm short of; I'll pay you for them when you get here. And about three cases of Extee Three. And some toys. Dr. Ortheris, you heard the tape, didn't you? Well, just think what you'd like to have if you were a Fuzzy, and bring it."

V

Victor Grego crushed out his cigarette slowly and deliberately.

"Yes, Leonard," he said patiently. "It's very interesting, and doubtless an important discovery, but I can't see why you're making such a production of it. Are you afraid I'll blame you for letting non-Company people beat you to it? Or do you merely suspect that anything Bennett Rainsford's mixed up in is necessarily a diabolical plot against the Company and, by consequence, human civilization?"

Leonard Kellogg looked pained. "What I was about to say, Victor, is that both Rainsford and this man Holloway seem convinced that these things they call Fuzzies aren't animals at all. They believe them to be sapient beings."

"Well, that's—" He bit that off short as the significance of what Kellogg had just said hit him. "Good God, Leonard! I beg your pardon abjectly; I don't blame you for taking it seriously. Why, that would make Zarathustra a Class-IV inhabited planet."

"For which the Company holds a Class-III charter," Kellogg added. "For an uninhabited planet."

Automatically void if any race of sapient beings were discovered on Zarathustra.

"You know what will happen if this is true?"

"Well, I should imagine the charter would have to be renegotiated, and now that the Colonial Office knows what sort of a planet this is, they'll be anything but generous with the Company. . . ."

"They won't renegotiate anything, Leonard. The Federation government will simply take the position that the Company has already made an adequate return on the original investments, and they'll award us what we can show as in our actual possession—I hope—and throw the rest into the public domain."

The vast plains on Beta and Delta continents, with their herds of veldbeest—all open range, and every 'beest that didn't carry a Company brand a maverick. And all the untapped mineral wealth, and the untilled arable land; it would take years of litigation even to make the Company's claim to Big Blackwater stick. And Terra-Baldur-Marduk Spacelines would lose their monopolistic franchise and get sticky about it in the courts, and in any case, the Company's import-export monopoly would go out the airlock. And the squatters rushing in and swamping everything—

"Why, we won't be any better off than the Yggdrasil Company, squatting on a guano heap on one continent!" he burst out. "Five years from now, they'll be making more money out of bat dung than we'll be making out of this whole world!"

And the Company's good friend and substantial stockholder, Nick Emmert, would be out, too, and a Colonial Governor General would move in, with regular army troops and a complicated bureaucracy. Elections, and a representative parliament, and every Tom, Dick and Harry with a grudge against the Company would be trying to get laws passed—And, of course, a Native Affairs Commission, with its nose in everything.

"But they couldn't just leave us without any kind of a charter," Kellogg insisted. Who was he trying to kid—besides himself? "It wouldn't be fair!" As though that clinched it. "It isn't our fault!"

He forced more patience into his voice. "Leonard, please try to realize that the Terran Federation government doesn't give one shrill soprano hoot on Nifflheim whether it's fair or not, or whose fault what is. The Federation government's been repenting that charter they gave the Company ever since they found out what they'd chartered away. Why, this planet is a better world than Terra ever was, even before the Atomic Wars. Now, if they have a chance to get it back, with improvements, you think they won't take it? And what will stop them? If those creatures over on Beta Continent are sapient beings, our charter isn't worth the parchment it's engrossed on, and that's an end of it." He was silent for a moment. "You heard that tape Rainsford transmitted to Jimenez. Did either he or Holloway actually claim, in so many words, that these things really are sapient beings?"

"Well, no; not in so many words. Holloway consistently alluded to them as people, but he's just an ignorant old prospector. Rainsford wouldn't come out and commit himself one way or another, but he left the door wide open for anybody else to."

"Accepting their account, could these Fuzzies be sapient?"

"Accepting the account, yes," Kellogg said, in distress. "They could be."

They probably were, if Leonard Kellogg couldn't wish the evidence out of existence.

"Then they'll look sapient to these people of yours who went over to Beta this morning, and they'll treat it purely as a scientific question and never consider the legal aspects. Leonard, you'll have to take charge of the investigation, before they make any reports everybody'll be sorry for."

Kellogg didn't seem to like that. It would mean having to exercise authority and getting tough with people, and he hated anything like that. He nodded very reluctantly.

"Yes. I suppose I will. Let me think about it for a moment, Victor."

One thing about Leonard; you handed him something he couldn't delegate or dodge and he'd go to work on it. Maybe not cheerfully, but conscientiously.

"I'll take Ernst Mallin along," he said at length. "This man Rainsford has no grounding whatever in any of the psychosciences. He may be able to impose on Ruth Ortheris, but not on Ernst Mallin. Not after I've talked to Mallin first." He thought some more. "We'll have to get these Fuzzies away from this man Holloway. Then we'll issue a report of discovery, being careful to give full credit to both Rainsford and Holloway—we'll even accept the designation they've coined for them—but we'll make it very clear that while highly intelligent, the Fuzzies are not a race of sapient beings. If Rainsford persists in making any such claim, we will brand it as a deliberate hoax.'"

"Do you think he's gotten any report off to the Institute of Xeno-Sciences yet?"

Kellogg shook his head. "I think he wants to trick some of our people into supporting his sapience claims; at least, corroborating his and Holloway's alleged observations.

46

That's why I'll have to get over to Beta as soon as possible."

By now, Kellogg had managed to convince himself that going over to Beta had been his idea all along. Probably also convincing himself that Rainsford's report was nothing but a pack of lies. Well, if he could work better that way, that was his business.

"He will, before long, if he isn't stopped. And a year from now, there'll be a small army of investigators here from Terra. By that time, you should have both Rainsford and Holloway thoroughly discredited. Leonard, you get those Fuzzies away from Holloway and I'll personally guarantee they won't be available for investigation by then. Fuzzies," he said reflectively. "Fur-bearing animals, I take it?"

"Holloway spoke, on the tape, of their soft and silky fur."

"Good. Emphasize that in your report. As soon as it's published, the Company will offer two thousand sols apiece for Fuzzy pelts. By the time Rainsford's report brings anybody here from Terra, we may have them all trapped out."

Kellogg began to look worried.

"But, Victor, that's genocide!"

"Nonsense! Genocide is defined as the extermination of a race of sapient beings. These are fur-bearing animals. It's up to you and Ernst Mallin to prove that."

The Fuzzies, playing on the lawn in front of the camp, froze into immobility, their faces turned to the west. Then they all ran to the bench by the kitchen door and scrambled up onto it.

"Now what?" Jack Holloway wondered.

"They hear the airboat," Rainsford told him. "That's the way they acted yesterday when you were coming in with your machine." He looked at the picnic table they had been spreading under the featherleaf trees. "Everything ready?"

"Everything but lunch; that won't be cooked for an hour yet. I see them now."

"You have better eyes than I do, Jack. Oh, I see it. I

hope the kids put on a good show for them," he said anxiously.

He'd been jittery ever since he arrived, shortly after breakfast. It wasn't that these people from Malorysport were so important themselves; Ben had a bigger name in scientific circles than any of this Company crowd. He was just excited about the Fuzzies.

The airboat grew from a barely visible speck, and came spiraling down to land in the clearing. When it was grounded and off contragravity, they started across the grass toward it, and the Fuzzies all jumped down from the bench and ran along with them.

The three visitors climbed down. Ruth Ortheris wore slacks and a sweater, but the slacks were bloused over a pair of ankle boots. Gerd van Riebeek had evidently done a lot of field work: his boots were stout, and he wore old, faded khakis and a serviceable-looking sidearm that showed he knew what to expect up here in the Piedmont. Juan Jimenez was in the same sports-casuals in which he had appeared on screen last evening. All of them carried photographic equipment. They shook hands all around and exchanged greetings, and then the Fuzzies began clamoring to be noticed. Finally all of them, Fuzzies and other people, drifted over to the table under the trees.

Ruth Ortheris sat down on the grass with Mamma and Baby. Immediately Baby became interested in a silver charm which she wore on a chain around her neck which tinkled fascinatingly. Then he tried to sit on her head. She spent some time gently but firmly discouraging this. Juan Jimenez was squatting between Mike and Mitzi, examining them alternately and talking into a miniature recorder phone on his breast, mostly in Latin. Gerd van Riebeek dropped himself into a folding chair and took Little Fuzzy on his lap.

"You know, this is kind of surprising," he said. "Not only finding something like this, after twenty-five years, but finding something as unique as this. Look, he doesn't have the least vestige of a tail, and there isn't another tailless mammal on the planet. Fact, there isn't another mammal on this planet that has the slightest kinship to him. Take ourselves; we belong to a pretty big family, about fifty-odd genera of primates. But this little fellow hasn't any relatives at all."

"Yeek?"

"And he couldn't care less, could he?" Van Riebeek pummeled Little Fuzzy gently. "One thing, you have the smallest humanoid known; that's one record you can claim. Oh-oh, what goes on?"

Ko-Ko, who had climbed upon Rainsford's lap, jumped suddenly to the ground, grabbed the chopper-digger he had left beside the chair and started across the grass. Everybody got to their feet, the visitors getting cameras out. The Fuzzies seemed perplexed by all the excitement. It was only another land-prawn, wasn't it?

Ko-Ko got in front of it, poked it on the nose to stop it and then struck a dramatic pose, flourishing his weapon and bringing it down on the prawn's neck. Then, after flopping it over, he looked at it almost in sorrow and hit it a couple of whacks with the flat. He began pulling it apart and eating it.

"I see why you call him Ko-Ko," Ruth said, aiming her camera. "Don't the others do it that way?"

"Well, Little Fuzzy runs along beside them and pivots and gives them a quick chop. Mike and Mitzi flop theirs over first and behead them on their backs. And Mamma takes a swipe at their legs first. But beheading and breaking the undershell, they all do that."

"Uh-huh; that's basic," she said. "Instinctive. The technique is either self-learned or copied. When Baby begins killing his own prawns, see if he doesn't do it the way Mamma does!"

"Hey, look!" Jimenez cried. "He's making a lobster pick for himself!"

Through lunch, they talked exclusively about Fuzzies. The subjects of the discussion nibbled things that were given to them, and yeeked among themselves. Gerd van Riebeek suggested that they were discussing the odd habits of human-type people. Juan Jimenez looked at him, slightly disturbed, as though wondering just how seriously he meant it.

"You know, what impressed me most in the taped account was the incident of the damnthing," said Ruth Ortheris. "Any animal associating with man will try to at-

49

tract attention if something's wrong, but I never heard of one, not even a Freyan kholph or a Terran chimpanzee, that would use descriptive pantomime. Little Fuzzy was actually making a symbolic representation, by abstracting the distinguishing characteristic of the damnthing."

"Think that stiff-arm gesture and bark might have been intended to represent a rifle?" Gerd Van Riebeek asked. "He'd seen you shooting before, hadn't he?"

"I don't think it was anything else. He was telling me, 'Big nasty damnthing outside; shoot it like you did the harpy.' And if he hadn't run past me and pointed back, that damnthing would have killed me."

Jimenez, hesitantly, said, "I know I'm speaking from ignorance. You're the Fuzzy expert. But isn't it possible that you're overanthropomorphizing? Endowing them with your own characteristics and mental traits?"

"Juan, I'm not going to answer that right now. I don't think I'll answer at all. You wait till you've been around these Fuzzies a little longer, and then ask it again, only ask yourself."

"So you see, Ernst, that's the problem."

Leonard Kellogg laid the words like a paperweight on the other words he had been saying, and waited. Ernst Mallin sat motionless, his elbows on the desk and his chin in his hands. A little pair of wrinkles, like parentheses, appeared at the corners of his mouth.

"Yes. I'm not a lawyer, of course, but . . ."

"It's not a legal question. It's a question for a psychologist."

That left it back with Ernst Mallin, and he knew it.

"I'd have to see them myself before I could express an opinion. You have that tape of Holloway's with you?" When Kellogg nodded, Mallin continued: "Did either of them make any actual, overt claim of sapience?"

He answered it as he had when Victor Grego had asked the same question, adding:

"The account consists almost entirely of Holloway's uncorroborated statements concerning things to which he claims to have been the sole witness."

"Ah." Mallin permitted himself a tight little smile. "And he's not a qualified observer. Neither, for that matter, is Rainsford. Regardless of his position as a xeno-naturalist, he is complete layman in the psychosciences. He's just taken this other man's statements uncritically. As for what he claims to have observed for himself, how do we know he isn't including a lot of erroneous inferences with his descriptive statements?"

"How do we know he's not perpetrating a deliberate hoax?"

"But, Leonard, that's a pretty serious accusation."

"It's happened before. That fellow who carved a Late Upland Martian inscription in that cave in Kenya, for instance. Or Hellermann's claim to have cross-bred Terran mice with Thoran tilbras. Or the Piltdown Man, back in the first century Pre-Atomic?"

Mallin nodded. "None of us like to think of a thing like that, but, as you say, it's happened. You know, this man Rainsford is just the type to do something like that, too. Fundamentally an individualistic egoist; badly adjusted personality type. Say he wants to make some sensational discovery which will assure him the position in the scientific world to which he believes himself entitled. He finds this lonely old prospector, into whose isolated camp'some little animals have strayed. The old man has made pets of them, taught them a few tricks, finally so projected his own personality onto them that he has convinced himself that they are people like himself. This is Rainsford's great opportunity; he will present himself as the discoverer of a new sapient race and bring the whole learned world to his feet." Mallin smiled again. "Yes, Leonard, it is altogether possible."

"Then it's our plain duty to stop this thing before it develops into another major scientific scandal like Hellermann's hybrids."

"First we must go over this tape recording and see what we have on our hands. Then we must make a thorough, unbiased study of these animals, and show Rainsford and his accomplice that they cannot hope to foist these ridiculous claims on the scientific world with impunity. If we can't convince them privately, there'll be nothing to do but expose them publicly."

"I've heard the tape already, but let's play it off now.

We want to analyze these tricks this man Holloway has taught these animals, and see what they show."

"Yes, of course. We must do that at once," Mallin said. "Then we'll have to consider what sort of statement we must issue, and what sort of evidence we will need to support it."

After dinner was romptime for Fuzzies on the lawn, but when the dusk came creeping into the ravine, they all went inside and were given one of their new toys from Mallorysport—a big box of many-colored balls and short sticks of transparent plastic. They didn't know that it was a molecule-model kit, but they soon found that the sticks would go into holes in the balls, and that they could be built into three-dimensional designs.

This was much more fun than the colored stones. They made a few experimental shapes, then dismantled them and began on a single large design. Several times they tore it down, entirely or in part, and began over again, usually with considerable yeeking and gesticulation.

"They have artistic sense," van Riebeek said. "I've seen lots of abstract sculpture that wasn't half as good as that job they're doing."

"Good engineering, too," Jack said. "They understand balance and center-of-gravity. They're bracing it well, and not making it top-heavy."

"Jack, I've been thinking about that question I was supposed to ask myself," Jimenez said. "You know, I came out here loaded with suspicion. Not that I doubted your honesty; I just thought you'd let your obvious affection for the Fuzzies lead you into giving them credit for more intelligence than they possess. Now I think you've consistently understated it. Short of actual sapience, I've never seen anything like them."

"Why short of it?" van Riebeek asked. "Ruth, you've been pretty quiet this evening. What do you think?"

Ruth Ortheris looked uncomfortable. "Gerd, it's too early to form opinions like that. I know the way they're working together looks like cooperation on an agreed-upon purpose, but I simply can't make speech out of that yeek-yeek-yeek."

"Let's keep the talk-and-build-a-fire rule out of it," van

Riebeek said. "If they're working together on a common project, they must be communicating somehow."

"It isn't communication, it's symbolization. You simply can't think sapiently except in verbal symbols. Try it. Not something like changing the spools on a recorder or field-stripping a pistol; they're just learned tricks. I mean ideas."

"How about Helen Keller?" Rainsford asked. "Mean to say she only started thinking sapiently after Anna Sullivan taught her what words were?"

"No, of course not. She thought sapiently—And she only thought in sense-imagery limited to feeling." She looked at Rainsford reproachfully; he'd knocked a breach in one of her fundamental postulates. "Of course, she had inherited the cerebroneural equipment for sapient thinking." She let that trail off, before somebody asked her how she knew that the Fuzzies hadn't.

"I'll suggest, just to keep the argument going, that speech couldn't have been invented without pre-existing sapience," Jack said.

Ruth laughed. "Now you're taking me back to college. That used to be one of the burning questions in first-year psych students' bull sessions. By the time we got to be sophomores, we'd realized that it was only an egg-and-chicken argument and dropped it."

"That's a pity," Ben Rainsford said. "It's a good question."

"It would be if it could be answered."

"Maybe it can be," Gerd said. "There's a clue to it, right there. I'll say that those fellows are on the edge of sapience, and it's an even-money bet which side."

"I'll bet every sunstone in my bag they're over."

"Well, maybe they're just slightly sapient," Jimenez suggested.

Ruth Ortheris hooted at that. "That's like talking about being just slightly dead or just slightly pregnant," she said. "You either are or you aren't."

Gerd van Riebeek was talking at the same time. "This sapience question is just as important in my field as yours, Ruth. Sapience is the result of evolution by natural selection, just as much as a physical characteristic, and it's the most important step in the evolution of any species, our own included."

"Wait a minute, Gerd," Rainsford said. "Ruth, what do you mean by that? Aren't there degrees of sapience?"

"No. There are degrees of mentation—intelligence, if you prefer—just as there are degrees of temperature. When psychology becomes an exact science like physics, we'll be able to calibrate mentation like temperature. But sapience is qualitatively different from nonsapience. It's more than just a higher degree of mental temperature. You might call it a sort of mental boiling point."

"I think that's a damn good analogy," Rainsford said. "But what happens when the boiling point is reached?"

"That's what we have to find out," van Riebeek told him. "That's what I was talking about a moment ago. We don't know any more about how sapience appeared today than we did in the year zero, or in the year 654 Pre-Atomic for that matter."

"Wait a minute," Jack interrupted. "Before we go any deeper, let's agree on a definition of sapience."

Van Riebeek laughed. "Ever try to get a definition of life from a biologist?" he asked. "Or a definition of number from a mathematician?"

"That's about it." Ruth looked at the Fuzzies, who were looking at their colored-ball construction as though wondering if they could add anything more without spoiling the design. "I'd say: a level of mentation qualitatively different from nonsapience in that it includes ability to symbolize ideas and store and transmit them, ability to generalize and ability to form abstract ideas. There; I didn't say a word about talk-and-build-a-fire, did I?"

"Little Fuzzy symbolizes and generalizes," Jack said. "He symbolizes a damnthing by three horns, and he symbolizes a rifle by a long thing that points and makes noises. Rifles kill animals. Harpies and damnthings are both animals. If a rifle will kill a harpy, it'll kill a damnthing too."

Juan Jimenez had been frowning in thought; he looked up and asked, "What's the lowest known sapient race?"

"Yggdrasil Khooghras," Gerd van Riebeek said promptly. "Any of you ever been on Yggdrasil?"

"I saw a man shot once on Mimir, for calling another man a son of a Khooghra," Jack said. "The man who shot him had been on Yggdrasil and knew what he was being called."

"I spent a couple of years among them," Gerd said. "They do build fires; I'll give them that. They char points on sticks to make spears. And they talk. I learned their language, all eighty-two words of it. I taught a few of the intelligentsia how to use machetes without maiming themselves, and there was one mental giant I could trust to carry some of my equipment, if I kept an eye on him, but I never let him touch my rifle or my camera."

"Can they generalize?" Ruth asked.

"Honey, they can't do nothin' else but! Every word in their language is a high-order generalization. *Hroosha,* live-thing. *Noosha,* bad-thing. *Dhishta,* thing-to-eat. Want me to go on? There are only seventy-nine more of them."

Before anybody could stop him, the communication screen got itself into an uproar. The Fuzzies all ran over in front of it, and Jack switched it on. The caller was a man in gray semiformals; he had wavy gray hair and a face that looked like Juan Jimenez's twenty years from now.

"Good evening; Holloway here."

"Oh, Mr. Holloway, good evening." The caller shook hands with himself, turning on a dazzling smile. "I'm Leonard Kellogg, chief of the Company's science division. I just heard the tape you made about the—the Fuzzies?" He looked down at the floor. "Are these some of the animals?"

"These are the Fuzzies." He hoped it sounded like the correction it was intended to be. "Dr. Bennett Rainsford's here with me now, and so are Dr. Jimenez, Dr. van Riebeek and Dr. Ortheris." Out of the corner of his eye he could see Jimenez squirming as though afflicted with ants, van Riebeek getting his poker face battened down and Ben Rainsford suppressing a grin. "Some of us are out of screen range, and I'm sure you'll want to ask a lot of questions. Pardon us a moment, while we close in."

He ignored Kellogg's genial protest that that wouldn't be necessary until the chairs were placed facing the screen. As an afterthought, he handed Fuzzies around, giving Little Fuzzy to Ben, Ko-Ko to Gerd, Mitzi to Ruth, Mike to Jimenez and taking Mamma and Baby on his own lap.

Baby immediately started to climb up onto his head, as expected. It seemed to disconcert Kellogg, also as expected. He decided to teach Baby to thumb his nose when given some unobtrusive signal.

"Now, about that tape I recorded last evening," he began.

"Yes, Mr. Holloway." Kellogg's smile was getting more mechanical every minute. He was having trouble keeping his eyes off Baby. "I must say, I was simply astounded at the high order of intelligence claimed for these creatures."

"And you wanted to see how big a liar I was. I don't blame you; I had trouble believing it myself at first."

Kellogg gave a musically blithe laugh, showing even more dental equipment.

"Oh, no, Mr. Holloway; please don't misunderstand me. I never thought anything like that."

"I hope not," Ben Rainsford said, not too pleasantly. "I vouched for Mr. Holloway's statements, if you'll recall."

"Of course, Bennett; that goes without saying. Permit me to congratulate you upon a most remarkable scientific discovery. An entirely new order of mammals—"

"Which may be the ninth extrasolar sapient race," Rainsford added.

"Good heavens, Bennett!" Kellogg jettisoned his smile and slid on a look of shocked surprise. "You surely can't be serious?" He looked again at the Fuzzies, pulled the smile back on and gave a light laugh.

"I thought you'd heard that tape," Rainsford said.

"Of course, and the things reported were most remarkable. But sapiences! Just because they've been taught a few tricks, and use sticks and stones for weapons—" He got rid of the smile again, and quick-changed to seriousness. "Such an extreme claim must only be made after careful study."

"Well, I won't claim they're sapient," Ruth Ortheris told him. "Not till day after tomorrow, at the earliest. But they very easily could be. They have learning and reasoning capacity equal to that of any eight-year-old Terran Human child, and well above that of the adults of some recognizedly sapient races. And they have not been taught tricks; they have learned by observation and reasoning."

"Well, Dr. Kellogg, mentation levels isn't my subject," Jimenez took it up, "but they do have all the physical characteristics shared by other sapient races—lower limbs

56

specialized for locomotion and upper limbs for manipulation, erect posture, stereoscopic vision, color perception, erect posture, hand with opposing thumb—all the characteristics we consider as prerequisite to the development of sapience."

"I think they're sapient, myself," Gerd van Riebeek said, "but that's not as important as the fact that they're on the very threshold of sapience. This is the first race of this mental level anybody's ever seen. I believe that study of the Fuzzies will help us solve the problem of how sapience developed in any race."

Kellogg had been laboring to pump up a head of enthusiasm; now he was ready to valve it off.

"But this is amazing! This will make scientific history! Now, of course, you all realize how pricelessly valuable these Fuzzies are. They must be brought at once to Mallorysport, where they can be studied under laboratory conditions by qualified psychologists, and—"

"No."

Jack lifted Baby Fuzzy off his head and handed him to Mamma, and set Mamma on the floor. That was reflex; the thinking part of his brain knew he didn't need to clear for action when arguing with the electronic image of a man twenty-five hundred miles away.

"Just forget that part of it and start over," he advised.

Kellogg ignored him. "Gerd,you have your airboat; fix up some nice comfortable cages—"

"Kellogg!"

The man in the screen stopped talking and stared in amazed indignation. It was the first time in years he had been addressed by his naked patronymic, and possibly the first time in his life he had been shouted at.

"Didn't you hear me the first time, Kellogg? Then stop gibbering about cages. These Fuzzies aren't being taken anywhere."

"But Mr. Holloway! Don't you realize that these little beings must be carefully studied? Don't you want them given their rightful place in the hierarchy of nature?"

"If you want to study them, come out here and do it. That's so long as you don't annoy them, or me. As far as study's concerned, they're being studied now. Dr. Rainsford's studying them, and so are three of your people, and when it comes to that, I'm studying them myself."

"And I'd like you to clarify that remark about qualified psychologists," Ruth Ortheris added, in a voice approaching zero-Kelvin. "You wouldn't be challenging my professional qualifications, would you?"

"Oh, Ruth, you know I didn't mean anything like that. Please don't misunderstand me," Kellogg begged. "But this is highly specialized work—"

"'Yes; how many Fuzzy specialists have you at Science Center, Leonard?" Rainsford wanted to know. "The only one I can think of is Jack Holloway, here."

"Well, I'd thought of Dr. Mallin, the Company's head psychologist."

"He can come too, just as long as he understands that he'll have to have my permission for anything he wants to do with the Fuzzies," Jack said. "When can we expect you?"

Kellogg thought some time late the next afternoon. He didn't have to ask how to get to the camp. He made a few efforts to restore the conversation to its original note of cordiality, gave that up as a bad job and blanked out. There was a brief silence in the living room. Then Jimenez said reproachfully:

"You certainly weren't very gracious to Dr. Kellogg, Jack. Maybe you don't realize it, but he is a very important man."

"He isn't important to me, and I wasn't gracious to him at all. It doesn't pay to be gracious to people like that. If you are, they always try to take advantage of it."

"Why, I didn't know you knew Len," van Riebeek said.

"I never saw the individual before. The species is very common and widely distributed." He turned to Rainsford. "You think he and this Mallin will be out tomorrow?"

"Of course they will. This is a little too big for underlings and non-Company people to be allowed to monkey with. You know, we'll have to watch out or in a year we'll be hearing from Terra about the discovery of a sapient race on Zarathustra; *Fuzzy fuzzy Kellogg*. As Juan says, Dr. Kellogg is a very important man. That's how he got important."

VI

The recorded voice ceased; for a moment the record player hummed voicelessly. Loud in the silence, a photocell acted with a double click, opening one segment of the sun shielding and closing another at the opposite side of the dome. Space Commodore Alex Napier glanced up from his desk and out at the harshly angular landscape of Xerxes and the blackness of airless space beyond the disquietingly close horizon. Then he picked up his pipe and knocked the heel out into the ashtray. Nobody said anything. He began packing tobacco into the bowl.

"Well, gentlemen?" He invited comment.

"Pancho?" Captain Conrad Greibenfeld, the Exec., turned to Lieutenant Ybarra, the chief psychologist.

"How reliable is this stuff?" Ybarra asked.

"Well, I knew Jack Holloway thirty years ago, on Fenris, when I was just an ensign. He must be past seventy now," he parenthesized. "If he says he saw anything, I'll believe it. And Bennett Rainsford's absolutely reliable, of course."

"How about the agent?" Ybarra insisted.

He and Stephen Aelborg, the Intelligence officer, exchanged glances. He nodded, and Aelborg said:

"One of the best. One of our own, lieutenant j.g., Naval Reserve. You don't need to worry about credibility, Pancho."

"They sound sapient to me," Ybarra said. "You know, this is something I've always been half hoping and half afraid would happen."

"You mean an excuse to intervene in that mess down there?" Greibenfeld asked.

Ybarra looked blankly at him for a moment. "No. No, I meant a case of borderline sapience; something our sacred talk-and-build-a-fire rule won't cover. Just how did this come to our attention, Stephen?"

"Well, it was transmitted to us from Contact Center in Mallorysport late Friday night. There seem to be a number of copies of this tape around; our agent got hold of one of them and transmitted it to Contact Center, and it was relayed on to us, with the agent's comments," Aelborg said. "Contract Center ordered a routine surveillance inside Company House and, to play safe, at the Residency. At the time, there seemed no reason to give the thing any beat-to-quarters-and-man-guns treatment, but we got a report on Saturday afternoon—Mallorysport time, that is—that Leonard Kellogg had played off the copy of the tape that Juan Jimenez had made for file, and had alerted Victor Grego immediately.

"Of course, Grego saw the implications at once. He sent Kellogg and the chief Company psychologist, Ernst Mallin, out to Beta Continent with orders to brand Rainsford's and Holloway's claims as a deliberate hoax. Then the Company intends to encourage the trapping of Fuzzies for their fur, in hopes that the whole species will be exterminated before anybody can get out from Terra to check on Rainsford's story."

"I hadn't heard that last detail before."

"Well, we can prove it," Aelborg assured him.

It sounded like a Victor Grego idea. He lit his pipe slowly. Damnit, he didn't want to have to intervene. No Space Navy C.O. did. Justifying intervention on a Colonial planet was too much bother—always a board of inquiry, often a courtmartial. And supersession of civil authority was completely against Service Doctrine. Of course, there were other and more important tenets of Service Doctrine. The sovereignty of the Terran Federation for one, and the inviolability of the Federation Constitution. And the rights of extraterrestrials, too. Conrad Greibenfeld, too, seemed to have been thinking about that.

"If those Fuzzies are sapient beings, that whole setup down there is illegal, Company, Colonial administration and all," he said. "Zarathustra's a Class-IV planet, and that's all you can make out of it."

"We won't intervene unless we're forced to. Pancho, I think the decision will be largely up to you."

Pancho Ybarra was horrified.

"Good God, Alex! You can't mean that. Who am I? A nobody. All I have is an ordinary M.D., and a Psych. D. Why, the best psychological brains in the Federation—"

"Aren't on Zarathustra, Pancho. They're on Terra, five hundred light-years away, six months' ship voyage each way. Intervention, of course, is my responsibility, but the sapience question is yours. I don't envy you, but I can't relieve you of it."

Gerd van Riebeek's suggestion that all three of the visitors sleep aboard the airboat hadn't been treated seriously at all. Gerd himself was accommodated in the spare room of the living hut. Juan Jimenez went with Ben Rainsford to his camp for the night. Ruth Ortheris had the cabin of the boat to herself. Rainsford was on the screen the next morning, while Jack and Gerd and Ruth and the Fuzzies were having breakfast; he and Jimenez had decided to take his airjeep and work down from the head of Cold Creek in the belief that there must be more Fuzzies around in the woods.

Both Gerd and Ruth decided to spend the morning at the camp and get acquainted with the Fuzzies on hand. The family had had enough breakfast to leave them neutral on the subject of land-prawns, and they were given another of the new toys, a big colored ball. They rolled it around in the grass for a while, decided to save it for their evening romp and took it into the house. Then they began playing aimlessly among some junk in the shed outside the workshop. Once in a while one of them would drift away to look for a prawn, more for sport than food.

Ruth and Gerd and Jack were sitting at the breakfast table on the grass, talking idly and trying to think of excuses for not washing the dishes. Mamma Fuzzy and Baby were poking about in the tall grass. Suddenly Mamma gave a shrill cry and started back for the shed, chasing Baby ahead of her and slapping him on the bottom with the flat of her chopper-digger to hurry him along.

Jack started for the house at a run. Gerd grabbed his camera and jumped up on the table. It was Ruth who saw the cause of the disturbance.

"Jack! Look, over there!" She pointed to the edge of the clearing. "Two strange Fuzzies!"

He kept on running, but instead of the rifle he had been going for, he collected his movie camera, two of the spare chopper-diggers and some Extee Three. When he emerged

61

again, the two Fuzzies had come into the clearing and stood side by side, looking around. Both were females, and they both carried wooden prawn-killers.

"You have plenty of film?" he asked Gerd. "Here, Ruth; take this." He handed her his own camera. "Keep far enough away from me to get what I'm doing and what they're doing. I'm going to try to trade with them."

He went forward, the steel weapons in his hip pocket and the Extee Three in his hand, talking softly and soothingly to the newcomers. When he was as close to them as he could get without stampeding them, he stopped.

"Our gang's coming up behind you," Gerd told him. "Regular skirmish line; choppers at high port. Now they've stopped, about thirty feet behind you."

He broke off a piece of Extee Three, put it in his mouth and ate it. Then he broke off two more pieces and held them out. The two Fuzzies were tempted, but not to the point of rashness. He threw both pieces within a few feet of them. One darted forward, threw a piece to her companion and then snatched the other piece and ran back with it. They stood together, nibbling and making soft delighted noises.

His own family seemed to disapprove strenuously of this lavishing of delicacies upon outsiders. However, the two strangers decided that it would be safe to come closer, and soon he had them taking bits of field ration from his hand. Then he took the two steel chopper-diggers out of his pocket, and managed to convey the idea that he wanted to trade. The two strange Fuzzies were incredulously delighted. This was too much for his own tribe; they came up yeeking angrily.

The two strange females retreated a few steps, their new weapon ready. Everybody seemed to expect a fight, and nobody wanted one. From what he could remember of Old Terran history, this was a situation which could develop into serious trouble. Then Ko-ko advanced, dragging his chopper-digger in an obviously pacific manner, and approached the two females, yeeking softly and touching first one and then the other. Then he laid his weapon down and put his foot on it. The two females began stroking and caressing him.

Immediately the crisis evaporated. The others of the

family came forward, stuck their weapons in the ground and began fondling the strangers. Then they all sat in a circle, swaying their bodies rhythmically and making soft noises. Finally Ko-Ko and the two females rose, picked up their weapons and started for the woods.

"Jack, stop them," Ruth called out. "They're going away."

"If they want to go, I have no right to stop them."

When they were almost at the edge of the woods, Ko-Ko stopped, drove the point of his weapon into the ground and came running back to Pappy Jack, throwing his arms around the human knees and yeeking. Jack stooped and stroked him, but didn't try to pick him up. One of the two females pulled his chopper-digger out, and they both came back slowly. At the same time, Little Fuzzy, Mamma Fuzzy, Mike and Mitzi came running back. For a while, all the Fuzzies embraced one another, yeeking happily. Then they all trooped across the grass and went into the house.

"Get that all, Gerd?" he asked.

"On film, yes. That's the only way I did, though. What happened?"

"You have just made the first film of intertribal social and mating customs, Zarathustran Fuzzy. This is the family's home; they don't want any strange Fuzzies hanging around. They were going to run the girls off. Then Ko-Ko decided he liked their looks, and he decided he'd team up with them. That made everything different; the family sat down with them to tell them what a fine husband they were getting and to tell Ko-Ko good-bye. Then Ko-Ko remembered that he hadn't told me good-bye, and he came back. The family decided that two more Fuzzies wouldn't be in excess of the carrying capacity of this habitat, seeing what a good provider Pappy Jack is, so now I should imagine they're showing the girls the family treasures. You know, they married into a mighty well-to-do family."

The girls were named Goldilocks and Cinderella. When lunch was ready, they were all in the living room, with the viewscreen on; after lunch, the whole gang went into the bedroom for a nap on Pappy Jack's bed. He spent the afternoon developing movie film, while Gerd and Ruth wrote up the notes they had made the day before and collaborated on an account of the adoption. By late afternoon, when they were finished, the Fuzzies came out for a frolic and prawn hunt.

They all heard the aircar before any of the human people did, and they all ran over and climbed up on the bench beside the kitchen door. It was a constabulary cruise car; it landed, and a couple of troopers got out, saying that they'd stopped to see the Fuzzies. They wanted to know where the extras had come from, and when Jack told them, they looked at one another.

"Next gang that comes along, call us and keep them entertained till we can get here," one of them said. "We want some at the post, for prawns if nothing else."

"What's George's attitude?" he asked. "The other night, when he was here, he seemed half scared of them."

"Aah, he's got over that," one of the troopers said. "He called Ben Rainsford; Ben said they were perfectly safe. Hey, Ben says they're not animals; they're people."

He started to tell them about some of the things the Fuzzies did. He was still talking when the Fuzzies heard another aircar and called attention to it. This time, it was Ben Rainsford and Juan Jimenez. They piled out as soon as they were off contragravity, dragging cameras after them.

"Jack, there are Fuzzies all over the place up there," Rainsford began, while he was getting out. "All headed down this way; regular *Volkerwanderung*. We saw over fifty of them—four families, and individuals and pairs. I'm sure we missed ten for every one we saw."

"We better get up there with a car tomorrow," one of the troopers said. "Ben, just where were you?"

"I'll show you on the map." Then he saw Goldilocks and Cinderella. "Hey! Where'd you two girls come from? I never saw you around here before."

There was another clearing across the stream, with a log footbridge and a path to the camp. Jack guided the big airboat down onto it, and put his airjeep alongside with the canopy up. There were two men on the forward deck of the boat, Kellogg and another man who would be Ernst Mallin. A third man came out of the control cabin after the boat was off contragravity. Jack didn't like Mallin. He had a tight, secretive face, with arrogance and bigotry showing underneath. The third man was younger. His face didn't show anything much, but his coat showed a bulge under the left arm. After being introduced by Kellogg, Mallin introduced him as Kurt Borch, his assistant.

Mallin had to introduce Borch again at the camp, not only to Ben Rainsford but also to van Riebeek, to Jimenez and even to Ruth Ortheris, which seemed a little odd. Ruth seemed to think so, too, and Mallin hastened to tell her that Borch was with Personnel, giving some kind of tests. That appeared to puzzle her even more. None of the three seemed happy about the presence of the constabulary troopers, either; they were all relieved when the cruise car lifted out.

Kellogg became interested in the Fuzzies immediately, squatting to examine them. He said something to Mallin, who compressed his lips and shook his head, saying:

"We simply cannot assume sapience until we find something in their behavior which cannot be explained under any other hypothesis. We would be much safer to assume nonsapience and proceed to test that assumption."

That seemed to establish the keynote. Kellogg straightened, and he and Mallin started one of those "of course I agree, doctor, but don't you find, on the other hand, that you must agree" sort of arguments, about the difference between scientific evidence and scientific proof. Jimenez got into it to the extent of agreeing with everything Kellogg said, and differing politely with everything Mallin said that he thought Kellogg woud differ with. Borch said nothing; he just stood and looked at the Fuzzies with ill-concealed hostility. Gerd and Ruth decided to help getting dinner.

They ate outside on the picnic table, with the Fuzzies watching them interestedly. Kellogg and Mallin carefully avoided discussing them. It wasn't until after dusk, when the Fuzzies brought their ball inside and everybody was in the living room, that Kellogg, adopting a presiding-officer manner, got the conversation onto the subject. For some time, without giving anyone else an opportunity to say anything, he gushed about what an important discovery the Fuzzies were. The Fuzzies themselves ignored him and began dismantling the stick-and-ball construction. For a while Goldilocks and Cinderella watched interestedly, and then they began assisting.

"Unfortunately," Kellogg continued, so much of our data is in the form of uncorroborated statements by Mr. Holloway. Now, please don't misunderstand me. I don't, myself, doubt for a moment anything Mr. Holloway said on that tape, but you must realize that professional scientists are most reluctant to accept the unsubstantiated reports of what, if you'll pardon me, they think of as nonqualified observers."

"Oh, rubbish, Leonard!" Rainsford broke in impatiently. "I'm a professional scientist, of a good many more years' standing than you, and I accept Jack Holloway's statements. A frontiersman like Jack is a very careful and exact observer. People who aren't don't live long on frontier planets."

"Now, please don't misunderstand me," Kellogg reiterated. "I don't doubt Mr. Holloway's statements. I was just thinking of how they would be received on Terra."

"I shouldn't worry about that, Leonard. The Institute accepts my reports, and I'm vouching for Jack's reliability. I can substantiate most of what he told me from personal observation."

"Yes, and there's more than just verbal statements," Gerd van Riebeek chimed in. "A camera is not a nonqualified observer. We have quite a bit of film of the Fuzzies."

"Oh, yes; there was some mention of movies," Mallin said. "You don't have any of them developed yet, do you?"

"Quite a lot. Everything except what was taken out in the woods this afternoon. We can run them off right now."

He pulled down the screen in front of the gunrack, got the film and loaded his projector. The Fuzzies, who had begun on a new stick-and-ball construction, were irritated when the lights went out, then wildly excited when Little Fuzzy, digging a toilet pit with the wood chisel, appeared. Little Fuzzy in particular was excited about that; if he didn't recognize himself, he recognized the chisel. Then there were pictures of Little Fuzzy killing and eating landprawns, Little Fuzzy taking the nut off the bolt and putting it on again, and pictures of the others, after they had

66

come in, hunting and at play. Finally, there was the film of the adoption of Goldilocks and Cinderella.

"What Juan and I got this afternoon, up in the woods, isn't so good, I'm afraid," Rainsford said when the show was over and the lights were on again. "Mostly it's rear views disappearing into the brush. It was very hard to get close to them in the jeep. Their hearing is remarkably acute. But I'm sure the pictures we took this afternoon will show the things they were carrying—wooden prawn-killers like the two that were traded from the new ones in that last film."

Mallin and Kellogg looked at one another in what seemed oddly like consternation.

"You didn't tell us there were more of them around," Mallin said, as though it were an accusation of duplicity. He turned to Kellogg. "This alters the situation."

"Yes, indeed, Ernst," Kellogg burbled delightedly. "This is a wonderful opportunity. Mr. Holloway, I understand that all this country up here is your property, by land-grant purchase. That's right, isn't it? Well, would you allow us to camp on that clearing across the run, where our boat is now? We'll get prefab huts—Red Hill's the nearest town, isn't it?—and have a Company construction gang set them up for us, and we won't be any bother at all to you. We had only intended staying tonight on our boat, and returning to Mallorysport in the morning, but with all these Fuzzies swarming around in the woods, we can't think of leaving now. You don't have any objection, do you?"

He had lots of objections. The whole business was rapidly developing into an acute pain in the neck for him. But if he didn't let Kellogg camp across the run, the three of them could move seventy or eighty miles in any direction and be off his land. He knew what they'd do then. They'd live-trap or sleep-gas Fuzzies; they'd put them in cages, and torment them with maze and electric-shock experiments, and kill a few for dissection, or maybe not bother killing them first. On his own land, if they did anything like that, he could do something about it.

"Not at all. I'll have to remind you again, though, that you're to treat these little people with consideration."

67

"Oh, we won't do anything to your Fuzzies," Mallin said.

"You won't hurt any Fuzzies. Not more than once, anyhow."

The next morning, during breakfast, Kellogg and Kurt Borch put in an appearance, Borch wearing old clothes and field boots and carrying his pistol on his belt. They had a list of things they thought they would need for their camp. Neither of them seemed to have more than the foggiest notion of camp requirements. Jack made some suggestions which they accepted. There was a lot of scientific equipment on the list, including an X-ray machine. He promptly ran a pencil line through that.

"We don't know what these Fuzzies' level of radiation tolerance is. We're not going to find out by overdosing one of my Fuzzies."

Somewhat to his surprise, neither of them gave him any argument. Gerd and Ruth and Kellogg borrowed his airjeep and started north; he and Borch went across the run to make measurements after Rainsford and Jimenez arrived and picked up Mallin. Borch took off soon after with the boat for Red Hill. Left alone, he loafed around the camp, and developed the rest of the movie film, making three copies of everything. Toward noon, Borch brought the boat back, followed by a couple of scowlike farmboats. In a few hours, the Company construction men from Red Hill had the new camp set up. Among other things, they brought two more airjeeps.

The two jeeps returned late in the afternoon, everybody excited. Between them, the parties had seen almost a hundred Fuzzies, and had found three camps, two among rocks and one in a hollow pool-ball tree. All three had been spotted by belts of filled-in toilet pits around them; two had been abandoned and the third was still occupied. Kellogg insisted on playing host to Jack and Rainsford for dinner at the camp across the run. The meal, because everything had been brought ready-cooked and only needed warming, was excellent.

Returning to his own camp with Rainsford, Jack found the Fuzzies finished with their evening meal and in the living room, starting a new construction—he could think of no other name for it—with the molecule-model balls and sticks. Goldilocks left the others and came over to him with a couple of balls fastened together, holding them up with one hand while she pulled his trouser leg with the other.

"Yes, I see. It's very beautiful," he told her.

She tugged harder and pointed at the thing the others were making. Finally, he understood.

"She wants me to work on it, too," he said. "Ben, you know where the coffee is; fix us a pot. I'm going to be busy here."

He sat down on the floor, and was putting sticks and balls together when Ben brought in the coffee. This was more fun than he'd had in a couple of days. He said so while Ben was distributing Extee Three to the Fuzzies.

"Yes, I ought to let you kick me all around the camp for getting this started," Rainsford said, pouring the coffee. "I could make some excuses, but they'd all sound like 'I didn't know it was loaded.' "

"Hell, I didn't know it was loaded, either." He rose and took his coffee cup, blowing on it to cool it. "What do you think Kellogg's up to, anyhow? That whole act he's been putting on since he came here is phony as a nine-sol bill."

"What I told you, evening before last," Rainsford said. "He doesn't want non-Company people making discoveries on Zarathustra. You notice how hard he and Mallin are straining to talk me out of sending a report back to Terra before he can investigate the Fuzzies? He wants to get his own report in first. Well, the hell with him! You know what I'm going to do? I'm going home, and I'm going to sit up all night getting a report into shape. Tomorrow morning I'm going to give it to George Lunt and let him send it to Mallorysport in the constabulary mail pouch. It'll be on a ship for Terra before any of this gang knows it's been sent. Do you have any copies of those movies you can spare?"

"About a mile and a half. I made copies of everything, even the stuff the others took."

"Good. We'll send that, too. Let Kellogg read about it in the papers a year from now." He thought for a moment, then said: "Gerd and Ruth and Juan are bunking at the other camp now; suppose I move in here with you tomorrow. I assume you don't want to leave the Fuzzies alone while that gang's here. I can help you keep an eye on them."

"But, Ben, you don't want to drop whatever else you're doing—"

"What I'm doing, now, is learning to be a Fuzzyologist, and this is the only place I can do it. I'll see you tomorrow, after I stop at the constabulary post."

The people across the run—Kellogg, Mallin and Borch, and van Riebeek, Jimenez and Ruth Ortheris—were still up when Rainsford went out to his airjeep. After watching him lift out, Jack went back into the house, played with his family in the living room for a while and went to bed. The next morning he watched Kellogg, Ruth and Jimenez leave in one jeep and, shortly after, Mallin and van Riebeek in the other. Kellogg didn't seem to be willing to let the three who had come to the camp first wander around unchaperoned. He wondered about that.

Ben Rainsford's airjeep came over the mountains from the south in the late morning and settled onto the grass. Jack helped him inside with his luggage, and then they sat down under the big featherleaf trees to smoke their pipes and watch the Fuzzies playing in the grass. Occasionally they saw Kurt Borch pottering around outside the other camp.

"I sent the report off," Rainsford said, then looked at his watch. "It ought to be on the mail boat for Mallorysport by now; this time tomorrow it'll be in hyperspace for Terra. We won't say anything about it; just sit back and watch Len Kellogg and Ernst Mallin working up a sweat trying to talk us out of sending it." He chuckled. "I made a definite claim of sapience; by the time I got the report in shape to tape off, I couldn't see any other alternative."

"Damned if I can. You hear that, kids?" he asked Mike and Mitzi, who had come over in hope that there might be goodies for them. "Uncle Ben says you're sapient."

"Yeek?"

"They want to know if it's good to eat. What'll happen now?"

"Nothing, for about a year. Six months from now, when the ship gets in, the Institute will release it to the press,

70

and then they'll send an investigation team here. So will any of the other universities or scientific institutes that may be interested. I suppose the government'll send somebody, too. After all, subcivilized natives on colonized planets are wards of the Terran Federation."

He didn't know that he liked that. The less he had to do with the government the better, and his Fuzzies were wards of Pappy Jack Holloway. He said as much.

Rainsford picked up Mitzi and stroked her. "Nice fur," he said. "Fur like that would bring good prices. It will, if we don't get these people recognized as sapient beings."

He looked across the run at the new camp and wondered. Maybe Leonard Kellogg saw that, too, and saw profits for the Company in Fuzzy fur.

The airjeeps returned in the middle of the afternoon, first Mallin's, and then Kellogg's. Everybody went inside. An hour later, a constabulary car landed in front of the Kellogg camp. George Lunt and Ahmed Khadra got out. Kellogg came outside, spoke with them and then took them into the main living hut. Half an hour later, the lieutenant and the trooper emerged, lifted their car across the run and set it down on the lawn. The Fuzzies ran to meet them, possibly expecting more whistles, and followed them into the living room. Lunt and Khadra took off their berets, but made no move to unbuckle their gun belts.

"We got your package off all right, Ben," Lunt said. He sat down and took Goldilocks on his lap; immediately Cinderella jumped up, also. "Jack, what the hell's that gang over there up to anyhow?"

"You got that, too?"

"You can smell it on them for a mile, against the wind. In the first place, that Borch. I wish I could get his prints; I'll bet we have them on file. And the whole gang's trying to hide something, and what they're trying to hide is something they're scared of, like a body in a closet. When we were over there, Kellogg did all the talking; anybody else who tried to say anything got shut up fast. Kellogg doesn't like you, Jack and he doesn't like Ben, and he doesn't like the Fuzzies. Most of all he doesn't like the Fuzzies."

"Well, I told you what I thought this morning," Rainsford said. "They don't want outsiders discovering things on this planet. It wouldn't make them look good to the home office on Terra. Remember, it was some non-Company people who discovered the first sunstones, back in 'Forty-eight."

George Lunt looked thoughtful. On him, it was a scowl.

"I don't think that's it, Ben. When we were talking to him, he admitted very freely that you and Jack discovered the Fuzzies. The way he talked, he didn't seem to think they were worth discovering at all. And he asked a lot of funny questions about you, Jack. The kind of questions I'd ask if I was checking up on somebody's mental competence." The scowl became one of anger now. "By God, I wish I had an excuse to question him—with a veridicator!"

Kellogg didn't want the Fuzzies to be sapient beings. If they weren't they'd be . . . fur-bearing animals. Jack thought of some overfed society dowager on Terra or Baldur, wearing the skins of Little Fuzzy and Mamma Fuzzy and Mike and Mitzi and Ko-Ko and Cinderella and Goldilocks wrapped around her adipose carcass. It made him feel sick.

VII

Tuesday dawned hot and windless, a scarlet sun coming up in a hard, brassy sky. The Fuzzies, who were in to wake Pappy Jack with their whistles, didn't like it; they were edgy and restless. Maybe it would rain today after all. They had breakfast outside on the picnic table, and then Ben decided he'd go back to his camp and pick up a few things he hadn't brought and now decided he needed.

"My hunting rifle's one," he said, "and I think I'll circle down to the edge of the brush country and see if I can pick off a zebralope. We ought to have some more fresh meat."

So, after eating, Rainsford got into his jeep and lifted away. Across the run, Kellogg and Mallin were walking back and forth in front of the camp, talking earnestly. When Ruth Ortheris and Gerd van Riebeek came out, they stopped, broke off their conversation and spoke briefly with them. Then Gerd and Ruth crossed the footbridge and came up the path together.

The Fuzzies had scattered, by this time, to hunt prawns. Little Fuzzy and Ko-Ko and Goldilocks ran to meet them; Ruth picked Goldilocks up and carried her, and Ko-Ko and Little Fuzzy ran on ahead. They greeted Jack, declining coffee; Ruth sat down in a chair with Goldilocks, Little Fuzzy jumped up on the table and began looking for goodies, and when Gerd stretched out on his back on the grass Ko-Ko sat down on his chest.

"Goldilocks is my favorite Fuzzy," Ruth was saying. "She is the sweetest thing. Of course, they're all pretty nice. I can't get over how affectionate and trusting they are; the ones we saw out in the woods were so timid."

"Well, the ones out in the woods don't have any Pappy Jack to look after them," Gerd said. "I'd imagine they're very affectionate among themselves, but they have so many things to be afraid of. You know, there's another prerequisite for sapience. It develops in some small, relatively defenseless, animal surrounded by large and dangerous enemies he can't outrun or outfight. So, to survive, he has to learn to outthink them. Like our own remote ancestors, or like Little Fuzzy; he had his choice of getting sapient or getting exterminated."

Ruth seemed troubled. "Gerd, Dr. Mallin has found absolutely nothing about them that indicates true sapience."

"Oh, Mallin be bloodied; he doesn't know what sapience is any more than I do. And a good deal less than you do, I'd say. I think he's trying to prove that the Fuzzies aren't sapient."

Ruth looked startled. "What makes you say that?"

"It's been sticking out all over him ever since he came here. You're a psychologist; don't tell me you haven't seen it. Maybe if the Fuzzies were proven sapient it would invalidate some theory he's gotten out of a book, and he'd have to do some thinking for himself. He wouldn't like that. But you have to admit he's been fighting the idea, intellectually and emotionally, right from the start. Why, they could sit down with pencils and slide rules and start working differential calculus and it wouldn't convince him."

"Dr. Mallin's trying to—" she began angrily. Then she broke it off. "Jack, excuse us. We didn't really come over here to have a fight. We came to meet some Fuzzies. Didn't we, Goldilocks?"

Goldilocks was playing with the silver charm on the chain around her neck, holding it to her ear and shaking it to make it tinkle, making small delighted sounds. Finally she held it up and said, "Yeek?"

"Yes, sweetie-pie, you can have it." Ruth took the chain from around her neck and put it over Goldilocks' head; she had to loop it three times before it would fit. "There now; that's your very own."

"Oh, you mustn't give her things like that."

"Why not. It's just cheap trade-junk. You've been on Loki, Jack, you know what it is." He did; he'd traded stuff like that to the natives himself. "Some of the girls at the hospital there gave it to me for a joke. I only wear it because I have it. Goldilocks likes it a lot better than I do."

An airjeep rose from the other side and floated across.

Juan Jimenez was piloting it; Ernst Mallin stuck his head out the window on the right, asked her if she were ready and told Gerd that Kellogg would pick him up in a few minutes. After she had gotten into the jeep and it had lifted out, Gerd put Ko-Ko off his chest and sat up, getting cigarettes from his shirt pocket.

"I don't know what the devil's gotten into her," he said, watching the jeep vanish. "Oh, yes, I do. She's gotten the Word from On High. Kellogg hath spoken. Fuzzies are just silly little animals," he said bitterly.

"You work for Kellogg, too, don't you?"

"Yes. He doesn't dictate my professional opinion, though. You know, I thought, in the evil hour when I took this job—" He rose to his feet, hitching his belt to balance the weight of the pistol on the right against the camera-binoculars on the left, and changed the subject abruptly. "Jack, has Ben Rainsford sent a report on the Fuzzies to the Institute yet?" he asked.

"Why?"

"If he hasn't, tell him to hurry up and get one in."

There wasn't time to go into that further. Kellogg's jeep was rising from the camp across the run and approaching.

He decided to let the breakfast dishes go till after lunch. Kurt Borch had stayed behind at the Kellogg camp, so he kept an eye on the Fuzzies and brought them back when they started to stray toward the footbridge. Ben Rainsford hadn't returned by lunchtime, but zebralope hunting took a little time, even from the air. While he was eating, outside, one of the rented airjeeps returned from the northeast in a hurry, disgorging Ernst Mallin, Juan Jimenez and Ruth Ortheris. Kurt Borch came hurrying out; they talked for a few minutes, and then they all went inside. A little later, the second jeep came in, even faster, and landed; Kellogg and van Riebeek hastened into the living hut. There wasn't anything more to see. He carried the dishes into the kitchen and washed them, and the Fuzzies went into the bedroom for their nap.

He was sitting at the table in the living room when Gerd van Riebeek knocked on the open door.

"Jack, can I talk to you for a minute?" he asked.

"Sure. Come in."

Van Riebeek entered, unbuckling his gun belt. He shifted a chair so that he could see the door from it, and laid the belt on the floor at his feet when he sat down. Then he began to curse Leonard Kellogg in four or five languages.

"Well, I agree, in principle; why in particular, though?"

"You know what that son of a Kooghra's doing?" Gerd asked. "He and that—" He used a couple of Sheshan words, viler than anything in Lingua Terra. "—that quack headshrinker, Mallin, are preparing a report, accusing you and Ben Rainsford of perpetrating a deliberate scientific hoax. You taught the Fuzzies some tricks; you and Rainsford, between you, made those artifacts yourselves and the two of you are conspiring to foist the Fuzzies off as sapient beings. Jack, if it weren't so goddamn stinking contemptible, it would be the biggest joke of the century!"

"I take it they wanted you to sign this report, too?"

"Yes, and I told Kellogg he could—" What Kellogg could do, it seemed, was both appalling and physiologically impossible. He cursed again, and then lit a cigarette and got hold of himself. "Here's what happened. Kellogg and I went up that stream, about twenty miles down Cold Creek, the one you've been working on, and up onto the high flat to a spring and a stream that flows down in the opposite direction. Know where I mean? Well, we found where some Fuzzies had been camping, among a lot of fallen timber. And we found a little grave, where the Fuzzies had buried one of their people."

He should have expected something like that, and yet it startled him. "You mean, they bury their dead? What was the grave like?"

"A little stone cairn, about a foot and a half by three, a foot high. Kellogg said it was just a big toilet pit, but I was sure of what it was. I opened it. Stones under the cairn, and then filled-in earth, and then a dead Fuzzy wrapped in grass. A female; she'd been mangled by something, maybe a bush-goblin. And get this Jack; they'd buried her prawn-stick with her."

"They bury their dead! What was Kellogg doing, while you were opening the grave?"

"Dithering around having ants. I'd been taking snaps of the grave, and I was burbling away like an ass about how

76

important this was and how it was positive proof of sapience, and he was insisting that we get back to camp at once. He called the other jeep and told Mallin to get to camp immediately, and Mallin and Ruth and Juan were there when we got in. As soon as Kellogg told them what we'd found, Mallin turned fish-belly white and wanted to know how we were going to suppress it. I asked him if he was nuts, and then Kellogg came out with it. They don't dare let the Fuzzies be proven sapient."

"Because the Company wants to sell Fuzzy furs?"

Van Riebeek looked at him in surprise. "I never thought of that. I doubt if they did, either. No. Because if the Fuzzies are sapient beings, the Company's charter is automatically void."

This time Jack cursed, not Kellogg but himself.

"I am a senile old dotard! Good Lord, I know colonial law; I've been skating on the edge of it on more planets than you're years old. And I never thought of that; why, of course it would. Where are you now, with the Company, by the way?"

"Out, but I couldn't care less. I have enough in the bank for the trip back to Terra, not counting what I can raise on my boat and some other things. Xeno-naturalists don't need to worry about finding jobs. There's Ben's outfit, for instance. And, brother, when I get back to Terra, what I'll spill about this deal!"

"If you get back. If you don't have an accident before you get on the ship." He thought for a moment. "Know anything about geology?"

"Why, some; I have to work with fossils. I'm as much a paleontologist as a zoologist. Why?"

"How'd you like to stay here with me and hunt fossil jellyfish for a while? We won't make twice as much, together, as I'm making now, but you can look one way while I'm looking the other, and we may both stay alive longer that way."

"You mean that, Jack?"

"I said it, didn't I?"

Van Riebeek rose and held out his hand; Jack came around the table and shook it. Then he reached back and picked up his belt, putting it on.

"Better put yours on, too, partner. Borch is probably the only one we'll need a gun for, but—"

Van Riebeek buckled on his belt, then drew his pistol and worked the slide to load the chamber. "What are we going to do?" he asked.

"Well, we're going to try to handle it legally. Fact is, I'm even going to call the cops."

He punched out a combination on the communication screen. It lighted and opened a window into the constabulary post. The sergeant who looked out of it recognized him and grinned.

"Hi, Jack. How's the family?" he asked. "I'm coming up, one of these evenings, to see them."

"You can see some now." Ko-Ko and Goldilocks and Cinderella were coming out of the hall from the bedroom; he gathered them up and put them on the table. The sergeant was fascinated. Then he must have noticed that both Jack and Gerd were wearing their guns in the house. His eyes narrowed slightly.

"You got problems, Jack?" he asked.

"Little ones; they may grow, though. I have some guests here who have outstayed their welcome. For the record, better make it that I have squatters I want evicted. If there were a couple of blue uniforms around, maybe it might save me the price of a few cartridges."

"I read you. George was mentioning that you might regret inviting that gang to camp on you." He picked up a handphone. "Calderon to Car Three," he said. "Do you read me, Three? Well, Jack Holloway's got a little squatter trouble. Yeah; that's it. He's ordering them off his grant, and he thinks they might try to give him an argument. Yeah, sure, Peace Lovin' Jack Holloway, that's him. Well, go chase his squatters for him, and if they give you anything about being Company big wheels, we don't care what kind of wheels they are, just so's they start rolling." He replaced the phone. "Look for them in about an hour, Jack."

"Why, thanks, Phil. Drop in some evening when you can hang up your gun and stay awhile."

He blanked the screen and began punching again. This time he got a girl, and then the Company construction boss at Red Hill.

"Oh, hello, Jack; is Dr. Kellogg comfortable?"

"Not very. He's moving out this afternoon. I wish you'd have your gang come up with those scows and get that stuff out of my back yard."

"Well, he told us he was staying for a couple of weeks."

"He got his mind changed for him. He's to be off my land by sunset."

The Company man looked troubled. "Jack, you haven't been having trouble with Dr. Kellogg, have you?" he asked. "He's a big man with the Company."

"That's what he tells me. You'll still have to come and get that stuff, though."

He blanked the screen. "You know," he said, "I think it would be no more than fair to let Kellogg in on this. What's his screen combination?"

Gerd supplied it, and he punched it out. One of those tricky special Company combinations. Kurt Borch appeared in the screen immediately.

"I want to talk to Kellogg."

"Doctor Kellogg is very busy, at present."

"He's going to be a damned sight busier; this is moving day. The whole gang of you have till eighteen hundred to get off my grant."

Borch was shoved aside, and Kellogg appeared. "What's this nonsense?" he demanded angrily.

"You're ordered to move. You want to know why? I can let Gerd van Riebeek talk to you; I think there are a few things he's forgotten to call you."

"You can't order us out like this. Why, you gave us permission—"

"Permission cancelled. I've called Mike Hennen in Red Hill; he's sending his scows back for the stuff he brought here. Lieutenant Lunt will have a couple of troopers here, too. I'll expect you to have your personal things aboard your airboat when they arrive."

He blanked the screen while Kellogg was trying to tell him that it was all a misunderstanding.

"I think that's everything. It's quite a while till sundown," he added, "but I move for suspension of rules while we pour a small libation to sprinkle our new partnership. Then we can go outside and observe the enemy."

There was no observable enemy action when they went out and sat down on the bench by the kitchen door. Kellogg would be screening Mike Hennen and the constabulary post for verification, and there would be a lot of gathering up and packing to do. Finally, Kurt Borch emerged with a contragravity lifter piled with boxes and luggage, and Jimenez walking beside to steady the load. Jimenez climbed up onto the airboat and Borch floated the load up to him and then went back into the huts. This was repeated several times. In the meantime, Kellogg and Mallin seemed to be having some sort of exchange of recriminations in front. Ruth Ortheris came out, carrying a briefcase, and sat down on the edge of a table under the awning.

Neither of them had been watching the Fuzzies, until they saw one of them start down the path toward the footbridge, a glint of silver at the throat identifying Goldilocks.

"Look at that fool kid; you stay put, Gerd, and I'll bring her back."

He started down the path; by the time he had reached the bridge, Goldilocks was across and had vanished behind one of the airjeeps parked in front of the Kellogg camp. When he was across and within twenty feet of the vehicle, he heard a sound across and within twenty feet of the vehicle, he heard a sound he had never heard before—a shrill, thin shriek, like a file on saw teeth. At the same time, Ruth's voice screamed.

"Don't! Leonard, stop that!"

As he ran around the jeep, the shrieking broke off suddenly. Goldilocks was on the ground, her fur reddened. Kellogg stood over her, one foot raised. He was wearing white shoes, and they were both spotted with blood. He stamped the foot down on the little bleeding body, and then Jack was within reach of him, and something crunched under the fist he drove into Kellogg's face. Kellogg staggered and tried to raise his hands; he made a strangled noise, and for an instant the idiotic thought crossed Jack's mind that he was trying to say, "Now, please don't misunderstand me." He caught Kellogg's shirt front in his left hand, and punched him again in the face, and again, and again. He didn't know how many times he punched Kellogg before he heard Ruth Ortheris' voice:

"Jack! Watch out! Behind you!"

He let go of Kellogg's shirt and jumped aside, turning and reaching for his gun. Kurt Borch, twenty feet away, had a pistol drawn and pointed at him.

His first shot went off as soon as the pistol was clear of the holster. He fired the second while it was still recoiling; there was a spot of red on Borch's shirt that gave him an aiming point for the third. Borch dropped the pistol he hadn't been able to fire, and started folding at the knees and then at the waist. He went down in a heap on his face.

Behind him, Gerd van Riebeek's voice was saying, "Hold it, all of you; get your hands up. You, too, Kellogg."

Kellogg, who had fallen, pushed himself erect. Blood was gushing from his nose, and he tried to stanch it on the sleeve of his jacket. As he stumbled toward his companions, he blundered into Ruth Ortheris, who pushed him angrily away from her. Then she went to the little crushed body, dropping to her knees beside it and touching it. The silver charm bell on the neck chain jingled faintly. Ruth began to cry.

Juan Jimenez had climbed down from the airboat; he was looking at the body of Kurt Borch in horror.

"You killed him!" he accused. A moment later, he changed that to "murdered." Then he started to run toward the living hut.

Gerd van Riebeek fired a bullet into the ground ahead of him, bringing him up short.

"You'll stop the next one, Juan," he said. "Go help Dr. Kellogg; he got himself hurt."

"Call the constabulary," Mallin was saying. "Ruth, you go; they won't shoot at you."

"Don't bother. I called them. Remember?"

Jimenez had gotten a wad of handkerchief tissue out of his pocket and was trying to stop his superior's nosebleed. Through it, Kellogg was trying to tell Mallin that he hadn't been able to help it.

"The little beast attacked me; it cut me with that spear it was carrying."

Ruth Ortheris looked up. The other Fuzzies were with her by the body of Goldilocks; they must have come as soon as they had heard the screaming.

"She came up to him and pulled at his trouser leg, the way they all do when they want to attract your attention," she said. "She wanted him to look at her new jingle." Her voice broke, and it was a moment before she could recover it. "And he kicked her, and then stamped her to death."

"Ruth, keep your mouth shut!" Mallin ordered. "The thing attacked Leonard; it might have given him a serious wound."

"It did!" Still holding the wad of tissue to his nose with one hand, Kellogg pulled up his trouser leg with the other and showed a scar on his shin. It looked like a briar scratch. "You saw it yourself."

"Yes, I saw it. I saw you kick her and jump on her. And all she wanted was to show you her new jingle."

Jack was beginning to regret that he hadn't shot Kellogg as soon as he saw what was going on. The other Fuzzies had been trying to get Goldilocks onto her feet. When they realized that it was no use, they let the body down again and crouched in a circle around it, making soft, lamenting sounds.

"Well, when the constabulary get here, you keep quiet," Mallin was saying. "Let me do the talking."

"Intimidating witnesses, Mallin?" Gerd inquired. "Don't you know everybody'll have to testify at the constabulary post under veridication? And you're drawing pay for being a psychologist, too." Then he saw some of the Fuzzies raise their heads and look toward the southeastern horizon. "Here come the cops, now."

However, it was Ben Rainsford's airjeep, with a zebra-lope carcass lashed along one side. It circled the Kelloggg camp and then let down quickly; Rainsford jumped out as soon as it was grounded, his pistol drawn.

"What happened, Jack?" he asked, then glanced around, from Goldilocks to Kellogg to Borch to the pistol beside Borch's body. "I get it. Last time anybody pulled a gun on you, they called it suicide."

"That's what this was, more or less. You have a movie camera in your jeep? Well, get some shots of Borch, and some of Goldilocks. Then stand by, and if the Fuzzies start

82

doing anything different, get it all. I don't think you'll be disappointed."

Rainsford looked puzzled, but he holstered his pistol and went back to his jeep, returning with a camera. Mallin began insisting that, as a licensed M.D., he had a right to treat Kellogg's injuries. Gerd van Riebeek followed him into the living hut for a first-aid kit. They were just emerging, van Riebeek's automatic in the small of Mallin's back, when a constabulary car grounded beside Rainsford's airjeep. It wasn't Car Three. George Lunt jumped out, unsnapping the flap of his holster, while Ahmed Khadra was talking into the radio.

"What's happened, Jack? Why didn't you wait till we got here?"

"This maniac assaulted me and murdered that man over there!" Kellogg began vociferating.

"Is your name Jack too?" Lunt demanded.

"My name's Leonard Kellogg, and I'm a chief of division with the Company—"

"Then keep quiet till I ask you something. Ahmed, call the post; get Knabber and Yorimitsu, with investigative equipment, and find out what's tying up Car Three."

Mallin had opened the first-aid kit by now; Gerd, on seeing the constabulary, had holstered his pistol. Kellogg, still holding the sodden tissues to his nose, was wanting to know what there was to investigate.

"There's the murderer; you have him red-handed. Why don't you arrest him?"

"Jack, let's get over where we can watch these people without having to listen to them," Lunt said. He glanced toward the body of Goldilocks. "That happen first?"

"Watch out, Lieutenant! He still has his pistol!" Mallin shouted warningly.

They went over and sat down on the contragravity-field generator housing one of the rented airjeeps. Jack started with Gerd van Riebeek's visit immediately after noon.

"Yes, I thought of that angle myself," Lunt said disgustedly. "I didn't think of it till this morning, though, and I didn't think things would blow up as fast as this. Hell, I just didn't think! Well, go on."

He interrupted a little later to ask: "Kellogg was stamping on the Fuzzy when you hit him. You were trying to stop him?"

"That's right. You can veridicate me on that if you want to."

"I will; I'll veridicate this whole damn gang. And this guy Borch had his heater out when you turned around? Nothing to it, Jack. We'll have to have some kind of a hearing, but it's just plain self-defense. Think any of this gang will tell the truth here, without taking them in and putting them under veridication?"

"Ruth Ortheris will, I think."

"Send her over here, will you."

She was still with the Fuzzies, and Ben Rainsford was standing beside her, his camera ready. The Fuzzies were still swaying and yeeking plaintively. She nodded and rose without speaking, going over to where Lunt waited.

"Just what did happen, Jack?" Rainsford wanted to know. "And whose side is he on?" He nodded toward van Riebeek, standing guard over Kellogg and Mallin, his thumbs in his pistol belt.

"Ours. He's quit the Company."

Just as he was finishing, Car Three put in an appearance; he had to tell the same story over again. The area in front of the Kellogg camp was getting congested; he hoped Mike Hennen's labor gang would stay away for a while. Lunt talked to van Riebeek when he had finished with Ruth, and then with Jimenez and Mallin and Kellogg. Then he and one of the men from Car Three came over to where Jack and Rainsford were standing. Gerd van Riebeek joined them just as Lunt was saying:

"Jack, Kellogg's made a murder complaint against you. I told him it was self-defense, but he wouldn't listen. So, according to the book, I have to arrest you."

"All right." He unbuckled his gun and handed it over. "Now, George, I herewith make complaint and accusation against Leonard Kellogg, charging him with the unlawful and unjustified killing of a sapient being, to wit, an aboriginal native of the planet of Zarathustra commonly known as Goldilocks."

Lunt looked at the small battered body and the six mourners around it.

"But, Jack, they aren't legally sapient beings."

"There is no such thing. A sapient being is a being on the mental level of sapience, not a being that has been declared sapient."

"Fuzzies are sapient beings," Rainsford said. "That's the opinion of a qualified xeno-naturalist."

"Two of them," Gerd van Riebeek said. "That is the body of a sapient being. There's the man who killed her. Go ahead, Lieutenant, make your pinch."

"Hey! Wait a minute!"

The Fuzzies were rising, sliding their chopper-diggers under the body of Goldilocks and lifting it on the steel shafts. Ben Rainsford was aiming his camera as Cinderella picked up her sister's weapon and followed, carrying it; the others carried the body toward the far corner of the clearing, away from the camp. Rainsford kept just behind them, pausing to photograph and then hurrying to keep up with them.

They set the body down. Mike and Mitzi and Cinderella began digging; the others scattered to hunt for stones. Coming up behind them, George Lunt took off his beret and stood holding it in both hands; he bowed his head as the grass-wrapped body was placed in the little grave and covered.

Then, when the cairn was finished, he replaced it, drew his pistol and checked the chamber.

"That does it, Jack," he said. "I am now going to arrest Leonard Kellogg for the murder of a sapient being."

VIII

Jack Holloway had been out on bail before, but never for quite so much. It was almost worth it, though, to see Leslie Coombes's eyes widen and Mohammed Ali O'Brien's jaw drop when he dumped the bag of sunstones, blazing with the heat of the day and of his body, on George Lunt's magisterial bench and invited George to pick out twenty-five thousand sols' worth. Especially after the production Coombes had made of posting Kellogg's bail with one of those precertified Company checks.

He looked at the whisky bottle in his hand, and then reached into the cupboard for another one. One for Gus Brannhard, and one for the rest of them. There was a widespread belief that that was why Gustavus Adolphus Brannhard was practicing sporadic law out here in the boon docks of a boon-dock planet, defending gun fighters and veldbeest rustlers. It wasn't. Nobody on Zarathustra knew the reason, but it wasn't whisky. Whisky was only the weapon with which Gus Brannhard fought off the memory of the reason.

He was in the biggest chair in the living room, which was none too ample for him; a mountain of a man with tousled gray-brown hair, his broad face masked in a tangle of gray-brown beard. He wore a faded and grimy bush jacket with clips of rifle cartridges on the breast, no shirt and a torn undershirt over a shag of gray-brown chest hair. Between the bottoms of his shorts and the tops of his ragged hose and muddy boots, his legs were covered with hair. Baby Fuzzy was sitting on his head, and Mamma Fuzzy was on his lap. Mike and Mitzi sat one on either knee. The Fuzzies had taken instantly to Gus. Bet they thought he was a Big Fuzzy.

"Aaaah!" he rumbled, as the bottle and glass were placed beside him. "Been staying alive for hours hoping for this."

"Well, don't let any of the kids get at it. Little Fuzzy

trying to smoke pipes is bad enough; I don't want any dipsos in the family, too."

Gus filled the glass. To be on the safe side, he promptly emptied it into himself.

"You got a nice family, Jack. Make a wonderful impression in court—as long as Baby doesn't try to sit on the judge's head. Any jury that sees them and hears that Ortheris girl's story will acquit you from the box, with a vote of censure for not shooting Kellogg, too."

"I'm not worried about that. What I want is Kellogg convicted."

"You better worry, Jack," Rainsford said. "You saw the combination against us at the hearing."

Leslie Coombes, the Company's top attorney, had come out from Mallorysport in a yacht rated at Mach 6, and he must have crowded it to the limit all the way. With him, almost on a leash, had come Mohammed Ali O'Brien, the Colonial Attorney General, who doubled as Chief Prosecutor. They had both tried to get the whole thing dismissed —self-defense for Holloway, and killing an unprotected wild animal for Kellogg. When that had failed, they had teamed in flagrant collusion to fight the inclusion of any evidence about the Fuzzies. After all it was only a complaint court; Lieutenant Lunt, as a police magistrate, had only the most limited powers.

"You saw how far they got, didn't you?"

"I hope we don't wish they'd succeeded," Rainsford said gloomily.

"What do you mean, Ben?" Brannhard asked. "What do you think they'll do?"

"I don't know. That's what worries me. We're threatening the Zarathustra Company, and the Company's too big to be threatened safely," Rainsford replied. "They'll try to frame something on Jack."

"With veridication? That's ridiciulous, Ben."

"Don't you think we can prove sapience?" Gerd van Riebeek demanded.

"Who's going to define sapience? And how?" Rainsford asked. "Why, between them, Coombes and O'Brien can even agree to accept the talk-and-build-a-fire rule."

"Huh-uh!" Brannhard was positive. "Court ruling on that, about forty years ago, on Vishnu. Infanticide case,

87

woman charged with murder in the death of her infant child. Her lawyer moved for dismissal on the grounds that murder is defined as the killing of a sapient being, a sapient being is defined as one that can talk and build a fire, and a newborn infant can do neither. Motion denied; the court ruled that while ability to speak and produce fire is positive proof of sapience, inability to do either or both does not constitute legal proof of nonsapience. If O'Brien doesn't know that, and I doubt if he does, Coombes will." Brannhard poured another drink and gulped it before the sapient beings around him could get at it. "You know what? I will make a small wager, and I will even give odds, that the first thing Ham O'Brien does when he gets back to Mallorysport will be to enter *nolle prosequi* on both charges. What I'd like would be for him to *nol. pros.* Kellogg and let the charge against Jack go to court. He would be dumb enough to do that himself, but Leslie Coombes wouldn't let him."

"But if he throws out the Kellogg case, that's it," Gerd van Riebeek said. "When Jack comes to trial, nobody'll say a mumblin' word about sapience."

"I will, and I will not mumble it. You all know colonial law on homicide. In the case of any person killed while in commission of a felony, no prosecution may be brought in any degree, against anybody. I'm going to contend that Leonard Kellogg was murdering a sapient being, that Jack Holloway acted lawfully in attempting to stop it and that when Kurt Borch attempted to come to Kellogg's assistance he, himself, was guilty of felony, and consequently any prosecution against Jack Holloway is illegal. And to make that contention stick, I shall have to say a great many words, and produce a great deal of testimony, about the sapience of Fuzzies."

"It'll have to be expert testimony," Rainsford said. "The testimony of psychologists. I suppose you know that the only psychologists on this planet are employed by the chartered Zarathustra Company." He drank what was left of his highball, looked at the bits of ice in the bottom of his glass and then rose to mix another one. "I'd have done the same as you did, Jack, but I still wish this hadn't happened."

"*Huh!*" Mamma Fuzzy looked up, startled by the exclamation. "What do you think Victor Grego's wishing, right now?"

Victor Grego replaced the hand-phone. "Leslie, on the yacht," he said. "They're coming in now. They'll stop at the hospital to drop Kellogg, and then they're coming here."

Nick Emmert nibbled a canape. He had reddish hair, pale eyes and a wide, bovine face.

"Holloway must have done him up pretty badly," he said.

"I wish Holloway'd killed him!" He blurted it angrily, and saw the Resident General's shocked expression.

"You don't really mean that, Victor?"

"The devil I don't! He gestured at the recorder-player, which had just finished the tape of the hearing, transmitted from the yacht at sixty-speeed. "That's only a teaser to what'll come out at the trial. You know what the Company's epitaph will be? *Kicked to death, along with ⌐ Fuzzy, by Leonard Kellogg.*"

Everything would have worked out perfectly if Kellogg had only kept his head and avoided collision with Holloway. Why, even the killing of the Fuzzy and the shooting of Borch, inexcusable as that had been, wouldn't have been so bad if it hadn't been for that asinine murder complaint. That was what had provoked Holloway's counter-complaint, which was what had done the damage.

And, now that he thought of it, it had been one of Kellogg's people, van Riebeek, who had touched off the explosion in the first place. He didn't know van Riebeek himself, but Kellogg should have, and he had handled him the wrong way. He should have known what van Riebeek would go along with and what he wouldn't.

"But, Victor, they won't convict Leonard of murder," Emmert was saying. "Not for killing one of those little things."

" 'Murder shall consist of the deliberate and unjustified killing of any sapient being, of any race,' " he quoted. "That's the law. If they can prove in court that the Fuzzies are sapient beings . . ."

Then, some morning, a couple of deputy marshals would take Leonard Kellogg out in the jail yard and put a bullet through the back of his head, which, in itself, would be no loss. The trouble was, they would also be shooting an irreparable hole in the Zarathustra Company's charter. Maybe Kellogg could be kept out of court, at that. There wasn't a ship blasted off from Darius without a couple of drunken spacemen being hustled aboard at the last moment; with the job Holloway must have done, Kellogg should look just right as a drunken spaceman. The twenty-five thousand sols' bond could be written off; that was pennies to the Company. No, that would still leave them stuck with the Holloway trial.

"You want me out of here when the others come, Victor?" Emmert asked, popping another canape into his mouth.

"No, no; sit still. This will be the last chance we'll have to get everybody together; after this, we'll have to avoid anything that'll look like collusion."

"Well, anything I can do to help; you know that, Victor," Emmert said.

Yes, he knew that. If worst came to utter worst and the Company charter were invalidated, he could still hang on here, doing what he could to salvage something out of the wreckage—if not for the Company, then for Victor Grego. But if Zarathustra were reclassified, Nick would be finished. His title, his social position, his sinecure, his grafts and perquisites, his alias-shrouded Company expense account—all out the airlock. Nick would be counted upon to do anything he could—however much that would be.

He looked across the room at the levitated globe, revolving imperceptibly in the orange spotlight. It was full dark on Beta Continent now, where Leonard Kellogg had killed a Fuzzy named Goldilocks and Jack Holloway had killed a gunman named Kurt Borch. That angered him, too; hell of a gunman! Clear shot at the broad of a man's back, and still got himself killed. Borch hadn't been any better choice than Kellogg himself. What was the matter with him; couldn't he pick men for jobs any more? And Ham O'Brien! No, he didn't have to blame himself for O'Brien. O'Brien was one of Nick Emmert's boys. And he hadn't picked Nick, either.

The squawk-box on the desk made a premonitory noise,

and a feminine voice advised him that Mr. Coombes and his party had arrived.

"All right; show them in."

Coombes entered first, tall, suavely elegant, with a calm, untroubled face. Leslie Coombes would wear the same serene expression in the midst of a bombardment or an earthquake. He had chosen Coombes for chief attorney, and thinking of that made him feel better. Mohammed Ali O'Brien was neither tall, elegant nor calm. His skin was almost black—he'd been born on Agni, under a hot B3 sun. His bald head glistened, and a big nose peeped over the ambuscade of a bushy white mustache. What was it they said about him? Only man on Zarathustra who could strut sitting down. And behind them, the remnant of the expedition to Beta Continent—Ernst Mallin, Juan Jimenez and Ruth Ortheris. Mallin was saying that it was a pity Dr. Kellogg wasn't with them.

"I question that. Well, please be seated. We have a great deal to discuss, I'm afraid."

Mr. Chief Justice Frederic Pendarvis moved the ashtray a few inches to the right and the slender vase with the spray of starflowers a few inches to the left. He set the framed photograph of the gentle-faced, white-haired woman directly in front of him. Then he took a thin cigar from the silver box, carefully punctured the end and lit it. Then, unabe to think of further delaying tactics, he drew the two bulky loose-leaf books toward him and opened the red one, the criminal-case docket.

Something would have to be done about this; he always told himself so at this hour. Shoveling all this stuff onto Central Courts had been all right when Mallorysport had had a population of less than five thousand and nothing else on the planet had had more than five hundred, but that time was ten years past. The Chief Justice of a planetary colony shouldn't have to wade through all this to see who had been accused of blotting the brand on a veldbeest calf or who'd taken a shot at whom in a barroom. Well, at least he'd managed to get a few misdemeanor and small-claims courts established; that was something.

The first case, of course, was a homicide. It usually was. From Beta, Constabulary Fifteen, Lieutenant George

Lunt. Jack Holloway—so old Jack had cut another notch on his gun—Cold Creek Valley, Federation citizen, race Terran human; willful killing of a sapient being, to wit Kurt Borch, Mallorysport, Federation citizen, race Terran human. Complainant, Leonard Kellogg, the same. Attorney of record for the defendant, Gustavus Adolphus Brannhard. The last time Jack Holloway had killed anybody, it had been a couple of thugs who'd tried to steal his sunstones; it hadn't even gotten into complaint court. This time he might be in trouble. Kellogg was a Company executive. He decided he'd better try the case himself. The Company might try to exert pressure.

The next charge was also homicide, from Constabulary, Beta Fifteen. He read it and blinked. Leonard Kellogg, willful killing of a sapient being, to wit, Jane Doe alias Goldilocks, aborigine, race Zarathustran Fuzzy; complainant, Jack Holloway, defendant's attorney of record, Leslie Coombes. In spite of the outrageous frivolity of the charge, he began to laugh. It was obviously an attempt to ridicule Kellogg's own complaint out of court. Every judicial jurisdiction ought to have at least one Gus Brannhard to liven things up a little. Race Zarathustra Fuzzy!

Then he stopped laughing suddenly and became deadly serious, like an engineer who finds a cataclysmite cartridge lying around primed and connected to a discharger. He reached out to the screen panel and began punching a combination. A spectacled young man appeared and greeted him deferentially.

"Good morning, Mr. Wilkins," he replied. "A couple of homicides at the head of this morning's docket—Holloway and Kellogg, both from Beta Fifteen. What is known about them?"

The young man began to laugh. "Oh, your Honor, they're both a lot of nonsense. Dr. Kellogg killed some pet belonging to old Jack Holloway, the sunstone digger, and in the ensuing unpleasantness—Holloway can be very unpleasant, if he feels he has to—this man Borch, who seems to have been Kellogg's bodyguard, made the suicidal error of trying to draw a gun on Holloway. I'm surprised at Lieutenant Lunt for letting either of those charges get past hearing court. Mr. O'Brien has entered *nolle prosequi* on both of them, so the whole thing can be disregarded."

Mohammed O'Brien knew a charge of cataclysmite when he saw one, too. His impulse had been to pull the detonator. Well, maybe this charge ought to be shot, just to see what it would bring down.

"I haven't approved the *nolle prosequi* yet, Mr. Wilkins," he mentioned gently. "Would you please transmit to me the hearing tapes on these cases, at sixty-speed? I'll take them on the recorder of this screen. Thank you."

He reached out and made the necessary adjustments. Wilkins, the Clerk of the Courts, left the screen, and returned. There was a wavering scream for a minute and a half. Going to take more time than he had expected. Well . . .

There wasn't enough ice in the glass, and Leonard Kellogg put more in. Then there was too much, and he added more brandy. He shouldn't have started drinking this early, be drunk by dinnertime if he kept it up, but what else was there to do? He couldn't go out, not with his face like this. In any case, he wasn't sure he wanted to.

They were all down on him. Ernst Mallin, and Ruth Ortheris, and even Juan Jimenez. At the constabulary post, Coombes and O'Brien had treated him like an idiot child who has to be hushed in front of company and coming back to Mallorysport they had ignored him completely. He drank quickly, and then there was too much ice in the glass again. Victor Grego had told him he'd better take a vacation till the trial was over, and put Mallin in charge of the division. Said he oughtn't to be in charge while the division was working on defense evidence. Well, maybe; it looked like the first step toward shoving him completely out of the Company.

He dropped into a chair and lit a cigarette. It tasted badly, and after a few puffs he crushed it out. Well, what else could he have done? After they'd found that little grave, he had to make Gerd understand what it would mean to the Company. Juan and Ruth had been all right, but Gerd—The things Gerd had called him; the things he'd said about the Company. And then that call from Holloway, and the humiliation of being ordered out like a tramp.

And then that disgusting little beast had come pulling

93

at his clothes, and he had pushed it away—well, kicked it maybe—and it had struck at him with the little spear it was carrying. Nobody but a lunatic would give a thing like that to an animal anyhow. And he had kicked it again, and it had screamed. . . .

The communication screen in the next room was buzzing. Maybe that was Victor. He gulped the brandy left in the glass and hurried to it.

It was Leslie Coombes, his face remotely expressionless.

"Oh, hello, Leslie."

"Good afternoon, Dr. Kellogg." The formality of address was studiously rebuking. "The Chief Prosecutor just called me; Judge Pendarvis has denied the *nolle prosequi* he entered in your case and in Mr. Holloway's, and ordered both cases to trial."

"You mean they're actually taking this seriously?"

"It is serious. If you're convicted, the Company's charter will be almost automatically voided. And, although this is important only to you personally, you might, very probably, be sentenced to be shot." He shrugged that off, and continued: "Now, I'll want to talk to you about your defense, for which I am responsible. Say ten-thirty tomorrow, at my office. I should, by that time, know what sort of evidence is going to be used against you. I will be expecting you, Dr. Kellogg."

He must have said more than that, but that was all that registered. Leonard wasn't really conscious of going back to the other room, until he realized that he was sitting in his relaxer chair, filling the glass with brandy. There was only a little ice in it, but he didn't care.

They were going to try him for murder for killing that little animal, and Ham O'Brien had said they wouldn't, he'd promised he'd keep the case from trial and he hadn't, they were going to try him anyhow and if they convicted him they would take him out and shoot him for just killing a silly little animal he had killed it he'd kicked it and jumped on it he could still hear it screaming and feel the horrible soft crunching under his feet. . . .

He gulped what was left in the glass and poured and gulped more. Then he staggered to his feet and stumbled over to the couch and threw himself onto it, face down, among the cushions.

Leslie Coombes found Nick Emmert with Victor Grego in the latter's office when he entered. They both rose to greet him, and Grego said "You've heard?"

"Yes. O'Brien called me immediately. I called my client —my client of record, that is—and told him. I'm afraid it was rather a shock to him."

"It wasn't any shock to me," Grego said as they sat down. "When Ham O'Brien's as positive about anything as he was about that, I always expect the worst."

"Pendarvis is going to try the case himself," Emmert said. "I always thought he was a reasonable man, but what's he trying to do now? Cut the Company's throat?"

"He isn't anti-Company. He isn't pro-Company either. He's just pro-law. The law says that a planet with native sapient inhabitants is a Class-IV planet, and has to have a Class-IV colonial government. If Zarathustra is a Class-IV planet, he wants it established, and the proper laws applied. If it's a Class-IV planet, the Zarathustra Company is illegally chartered. It's his job to put a stop to illegality. Frederic Pendarvis' religion is the law, and he is its priest. You never get anywhere by arguing religion with a priest."

They were both silent for a while after he had finished. Grego was looking at the globe, and he realized, now, that while he was proud of it, his pride was the pride in a paste jewel that stands for a real one in a bank vault. Now he was afraid that the real jewel was going to be stolen from him. Nick Emmert was just afraid.

"You were right yesterday, Victor. I wish Holloway'd killed that son of a Khooghra. Maybe it's not too late—"

"Yes, it is, Nick. It's too late to do anything like that. It's too late to do anything but win the case in court." He turned to Grego. "What are your people doing?"

Grego took his eyes from the globe. "Ernst Mallin's studying all the filmed evidence we have and all the descriptions of Fuzzy behavior, and trying to prove that none of it is the result of sapient mentation. Ruth Ortheris is doing the same, only she's working on the line of instinct and conditioned reflexes and nonsapient, single-stage reasoning. She has a lot of rats, and some dogs and monkeys, and a lot of apparatus, and some technician from Henry Stenson's instrument shop helping her. Juan Jimenez is studying mentation of Terran dogs, cats and primates, and Freyan kholphs and Mimir black slinkers."

"He hasn't turned up any simian or canine parallels to that funeral, has he?"

Grego said nothing; merely shook his head. Emmert muttered something inaudible and probably indecent.

"I didn't think he had. I only hope those Fuzzies don't get up in court, build a bonfire and start making speeches in Lingua Terra."

Nick Emmert cried out in panic. "You believe they're sapient yourself!"

"Of course. Don't you?"

Grego laughed sourly. "Nick thinks you have to believe a thing to prove it. It helps, but it isn't necessary. Say we're a debating team; we've been handed the negative of the question. *Resolved: that Fuzzies are Sapient Beings.* Personally, I think we have the short end of it, but that only means we'll have to work harder on it."

"You know, I was on a debating team at college," Emmert said brightly. When that was disregarded, he added: "If I remember, the first thing was definition of terms."

Grego looked up quickly. "Leslie, I think Nick has something. What is the legal definition of a sapient being?"

"As far as I know, there isn't any. Sapience is something that's just taken for granted."

"How about talk-and-build-a-fire?"

He shook his head. *"People of the Colony of Vishnu versus Emily Morrosh, 612 A.E."* He told them about the infanticide case. "I was looking up rulings on sapience; I passed the word on to Ham O'Brien. You know, what your people will have to do will be to produce a definition of sapience, acceptable to the court, that will include all known sapient races and at the same time exclude the Fuzzies. I don't envy them."

"We need some Fuzzies of our own to study," Grego said.

"Too bad we can't get hold of Holloway's," Emmert said. "Maybe we could, if he leaves them alone at his camp."

"No. We can't risk that." He thought for a moment. "Wait a moment. I think we might be able to do it at that. Legally."

IX

Jack Holloway saw Little Fuzzy eying the pipe he had laid in the ashtray, and picked it up, putting it in his mouth. Little Fuzzy looked reproachfully at him and started to get down onto the floor. Pappy Jack was mean; didn't he think a Fuzzy might want to smoke a pipe, too? Well, maybe it wouldn't hurt him. He picked Little Fuzzy up and set him back on his lap, offering the pipestem. Little Fuzzy took a puff. He didn't cough over it; evidently he had learned how to avoid inhaling.

"They scheduled the Kellogg trial first," Gus Brannhard was saying, "and there wasn't any way I could stop that. You see what the idea is? They'll try him first, with Leslie Coombes running both the prosecution and the defense, and if they can get him acquitted, it'll prejudice the sapience evidence we introduce in your trial."

Mamma Fuzzy made another try at intercepting the drink he was hoisting, but he frustrated that. Baby had stopped trying to sit on his head, and was playing peek-a-boo from behind his whiskers.

"First," he continued, "they'll exclude every bit of evidence about the Fuzzies that they can. That won't be much, but there'll be a fight to get any of it in. What they can't exclude, they'll attack. They'll attack credibility. Of course, with veridication, they can't claim anybody's lying, but they can claim self-deception. You make a statement you believe, true or false, and the veridicator'll back you up on it. They'll attack qualifications on expert testimony. They'll quibble about statements of fact and statements of opinion. And what they can't exclude or attack, they'll accept, and then deny that it's proof of sapience."

"What the hell do they want for proof of sapience?" Gerd demanded. "Nuclear energy and contragravity and hyperdrive?"

"They will have a nice, neat, pedantic definition of sapience, tailored especially to exclude the Fuzzies, and they will present it in court and try to get it accepted, and it's up to us to guess in advance what that will be, and have a refutation of it ready, and also a definition of our own."

"Their definition will have to include Khooghras. Gerd, do the Khooghras bury their dead?"

"Hell, no; they eat them. But you have to give them this, they cook them first."

"Look, we won't get anywhere arguing about what Fuzzies do and Khooghras don't do," Rainsford said. "We'll have to get a definition of sapience. Remember what Ruth said Saturday night?"

Gerd van Riebeek looked as though he didn't want to remember what Ruth had said, or even remember Ruth herself. Jack nodded, and repeated it. "I got the impression of non-sapient intelligence shading up to a sharp line, and then sapience shading up from there, maybe a different color, or wavy lines instead of straight ones."

"That's a good graphic representation," Gerd said. "You know, that line's so sharp I'd be tempted to think of sapience as a result of mutation, except that I can't quite buy the same mutation happening in the same way on so many different planets."

Ben Rainsford started to say something, then stopped short when a constabulary siren hooted over the camp. The Fuzzies looked up interestedly. They knew what that was. Pappy Jack's friends in the blue clothes. Jack went to the door and opened it, putting the outside light on.

The car was landing; George Lunt, two of his men and two men in civilian clothes were getting out. Both the latter were armed, and one of them carried a bundle under his arm.

"Hello, George; come on in."

"We want to talk to you, Jack." Lunt's voice was strained, empty of warmth or friendliness. "At least, these men do."

"Why, yes. Sure."

He backed into the room to permit them to enter. Something was wrong; something bad had come up. Khadra came in first, placing himself beside and a little behind him. Lunt followed, glancing quickly around and placing himself between Jack and the gunrack and also the holstered pistols on the table. The third trooper let the two strangers in ahead of him, and then closed the door and put his back against it. He wondered if the court might have cancelled his bond and ordered him into custody. The two strangers—a beefy man with a scrubby black mustache and a smaller one with a thin, saturnine face—were looking expectantly at Lunt. Rainsford and van Riebeek were on their feet. Gus Brannhard leaned over to refill his glass, but did not rise.

"Let me have the papers," Lunt said to the beefy stranger.

The other took a folded document and handed it over.

"Jack, this isn't my idea," Lunt said. "I don't want to do it, but I have to. I wouldn't want to shoot you, either, but you make any resistance and I will. I'm no Kurt Borch; I know you, and I won't take any chances."

"If you're going to serve that paper, serve it," the bigger of the two strangers said. "Don't stand yakking all night."

"Jack," Lunt said uncomfortably, "this is a court order to impound your Fuzzies as evidence in the Kellogg case. These men are deputy marshals from Central Courts; they've been ordered to bring the Fuzzies into Mallorysport."

"Let me see the order, Jack," Brannhard said, still remaining seated.

Lunt handed it to Jack, and he handed it across to Brannhard. Gus had been drinking steadily all evening; maybe he was afraid he'd show it if he stood up. He looked at it briefly and nodded.

"Court order, all right, signed by the Chief Justice." He handed it back. "They have to take the Fuzzies, and that's all there is to it. Keep that order, though, and make them give you a signed and thumbprinted receipt. Type it up for them now, Jack."

Gus wanted to busy him with something, so he wouldn't have to watch what was going on. The smaller of the two deputies had dropped the bundle from under his arm. It was a number of canvas sacks. He sat down at the typewriter, closing his ears to the noises in the room, and wrote the receipt, naming the Fuzzies and describing them, and specifying that they were in good health and uninjured. One of them tried to climb to his lap, yeeking frantically; it clutched his shirt, but it was snatched away. He was finished with his work before the invaders were with theirs. They had three Fuzzies already in sacks. Khadra was catching Cinderella. Ko-Ko and Little Fuzzy had run for the little door in the outside wall, but Lunt was standing with his heels against it, holding it shut; when they saw that, both of them began burrowing in the bedding. The third trooper and the smaller of the two deputies dragged them out and stuffed them into sacks.

He got to his feet, still stunned and only half comprehending, and took the receipt out of the typewriter. There was an argument about it; Lunt told the deputies to sign it or get the hell out without the Fuzzies. They signed, inked their thumbs and printed after their signatures. Jack gave the paper to Gus, trying not to look at the six bulging, writhing sacks, or hear the frightened little sounds.

"George, you'll let them have some of their things, won't you?" he asked.

"Sure. What kind of things?"

"Their bedding. Some of their toys."

"You mean this junk?" The smaller of the two deputies kicked the ball-and-stick construction. "All we got orders to take is the Fuzzies."

"You heard the gentleman." Lunt made the word sound worse than son of a Khooghra. He turned to the two deputies. "Well, you have them; what are you waiting for?"

Jack watched from the door as they put the sacks into the aircar, climbed in after them and lifted out. Then he came back and sat down at the table.

"They don't know anything about court orders," he said. "They don't know why I didn't stop it. They think Pappy Jack let them down."

"Have they gone, Jack?" Brannhard asked. "Sure?" Then he rose, reaching behind him, and took up a little ball of white fur. Baby Fuzzy caught his beard with both tiny hands, yeeking happily.

"Baby! They didn't get him!"

Brannhard disengaged the little hands from his beard and handed him over.

"No, and they signed for him, too." Brannhard downed what was left of his drink, got a cigar out of his pocket and lit it. "Now, we're going to go to Mallorysport and get the rest of them back."

100

"But . . . But the Chief Justice signed that order. He won't give them back just because we ask him to."

Brannhard made an impolite noise. "I'll bet everything I own Pendarvis never saw that order. They have stacks of those things, signed in blank, in the Chief of the Court's office. If they had to wait to get one of the judges to sign an order every time they wanted to subpoena a witness or impound physical evidence, they'd never get anything done. If Ham O'Brien didn't think this up for himself, Leslie Coombes thought it up for him."

"We'll use my airboat," Gerd said. "You coming along, Ben? Let's get started."

He couldn't understand. The Big Ones in the blue clothes had been friends; they had given the whistles, and shown sorrow when the killed one was put in the ground. And why had Pappy Jack not gotten the big gun and stopped them. It couldn't be that he was afraid; Pappy Jack was afraid of nothing.

The others were near, in bags like the one in which he had been put; he could hear them, and called to them. Then he felt the edge of the little knife Pappy Jack had made. He could cut his way out of this bag now and free the others, but that would be no use. They were in one of the things the Big Ones went up into the sky in, and if he got out now, there would be nowhere to go and they would be caught at once. Better to wait.

The one thing that really worried him was that he would not know where they were being taken. When they did get away, how would they ever find Pappy Jack again?

Gus Brannhard was nervous, showing it by being over-talkative, and that worried Jack. He'd stopped twice at mirrors along the hallway to make sure that his gold-threaded gray neckcloth was properly knotted and that his black jacket was zipped up far enough and not too far. Now, in front of the door marked THE CHIEF JUSTICE, he paused before pushing the button to fluff his newly shampooed beard.

There were two men in the Chief Justice's private chambers. Pendarvis he had seen once or twice, but their

101

paths had never crossed. He had a good face, thin and ascetic, the face of a man at peace with himself. With him was Mohammed Ali O'Brien, who seemed surprised to see them enter, and then apprehensive. Nobody shook hands; the Chief Justice bowed slightly and invited them to be seated.

"Now," he continued, when they found chairs, "Miss Ugatori tells me that you are making complaint against an action by Mr. O'Brien here."

"We are indeed, your Honor." Brannhard opened his briefcase and produced two papers—the writ, and the receipt for the Fuzzies, handing them across the desk. "My client and I wish to know upon what basis of legality your Honor sanctioned this act, and by what right Mr. O'Brien sent his officers to Mr. Holloway's camp to snatch these little people from their friend and protector, Mr. Holloway."

The judge looked at the two papers. "As you know, Miss Ugatori took prints of them when you called to make this appointment. I've seen them. But believe me, Mr. Brannhard, this is the first time I have seen the original of this writ. You know how these things are signed in blank. It's a practice that has saved considerable time and effort, and until now they have only been used when there was no question that I or any other judge would approve. Such a question should certainly have existed in this case, because had I seen this writ I would never have signed it." He turned to the now fidgeting Chief Prosecutor. "Mr. O'Brien," he said, "one simply does not impound sapient beings as evidence, as, say, one impounds a veldbeest calf in a brand-alteration case. The fact that the sapience of these Fuzzies is still *sub judice* includes the presumption of its possibility. Now you know perfectly well that the courts may take no action in the face of the possibility that some innocent person may suffer wrong."

"And, your Honor," Brannhard leaped into the breach, "it cannot be denied that these Fuzzies have suffered a most outrageous wrong! Picture them—no, picture innocent and artless children, for that is what these Fuzzies are, happy, trusting little children, who, until then, had known only kindness and affection—rudely kidnaped, stuffed into sacks by brutal and callous men—"

102

"Your Honor!" O'Brien's face turned even blacker than the hot sun of Agni had made it. "I cannot hear officers of the court so characterized without raising my voice in protest!"

"Mr. O'Brien seems to forget that he is speaking in the presence of two eye witnesses to this brutal abduction."

"If the officers of the court need defense, Mr. O'Brien, the court will defend them. I believe that you should presently consider a defense of your own actions."

"Your Honor, I insist that I only acted as I felt to be my duty," O'Brien said. "These Fuzzies are a key exhibit in the case of *People* versus *Kellogg,* since only by demonstration of their sapience can any prosecution against the defendant be maintained."

"Then why," Brannhard demanded, "did you endanger them in this criminally reckless manner?"

"Endanger them?" O'Brien was horrified. "Your Honor, I acted only to insure their safety and appearance in court."

"So you took them away from the only man on this planet who knows anything about their proper care, a man who loves them as he would his own human children, and you subjected them to abuse which, for all you knew, might have been fatal to them."

Judge Pendarvis nodded. "I don't believe, Mr. Brannhard, that you have overstated the case. Mr. O'Brien, I take a very unfavorable view of your action in this matter. You had no right to have what are at least putatively sapient beings treated in this way, and even viewing them as mere physical evidence I must agree with Mr. Brannhard's characterization of your conduct as criminally reckless. Now, speaking judicially, I order you to produce those Fuzzies immediately and return them to the custody of Mr. Holloway."

"Well, of course, your Honor." O'Brien had been growing progressively distraught, and his face now had the gray-over-brown hue of a walnut gunstock that has been out in the rain all day. "It'll take an hour or so to send for them and have them brought here."

"You mean they're not in this building?" Pendarvis asked.

"Oh, no, your Honor, there are no facilities here. I had them taken to Science Center—"

"What?"

Jack had determined to keep his mouth shut and let Gus do the talking. The exclamation was literally forced out of him. Nobody noticed; it had also been forced out of both Gus Brannhard and Judge Pendarvis. Pendarvis leaned forward and spoke with dangerous mildness:

"Do you refer, Mr. O'Brien, to the establishment of the Division of Scientific Study and Research of the chartered Zarathustra Company?"

"Why, yes; they have facilities for keeping all kinds of live animals, and they do all the scientific work for—"

Pendarvis cursed blasphemously. Brannhard looked as startled as though his own briefcase had jumped at his throat and tried to bite him. He didn't look half as startled as Ham O'Brien did.

"So you think," Pendarvis said, recovering his composure with visible effort, "that the logical custodian of prosecution evidence in a murder trial is the defendant? Mr. O'Brien, you simply enlarge my view of the possible!"

"The Zarathustra Company isn't the defendant," O'Brien argued sullenly.

"Not of record, no," Brannhard agreed. "But isn't the Zarathustra Company's scientific division headed by one Leonard Kellogg?"

"Dr. Kellogg's been relieved of his duties, pending the outcome of the trial. The division is now headed by Dr. Ernst Mallin."

"Chief scientific witness for the defense; I fail to see any practical difference."

"Well, Mr. Emmert said it would be all right," O'Brien mumbled.

"Jack, did you hear that?" Brannhard asked. "Treasure it in your memory. You may have to testify to it in court sometime." He turned to the Chief Justice. "Your Honor, may I suggest the recovery of these Fuzzies be entrusted to Colonial Marshal Fane, and may I further suggest that Mr. O'Brien be kept away from any communication equipment until they are recovered."

"That sounds like a prudent suggestion, Mr. Brannhard.

104

Now, I'll give you an order for the surrender of the Fuzzies, and a search warrant, just to be on the safe side. And, I think, an Orphans' Court from naming Mr. Holloway as guardian of these putatively sapient beings. What are their names? Oh, I have them here on this receipt." He smiled pleasantly. "See, Mr. O'Brien, we're saving you a lot of trouble."

O'Brien had little enough wit to protest. "But these are the defendant and his attorney in another murder case I'm prosecuting," he began.

Pendarvis stopped smiling. "Mr. O'Brien, I doubt if you'll be allowed to prosecute anything or anybody around here any more, and I am specifically relieving you of any connection with either the Kellogg or the Holloway trial, and if I hear any argument out of you about it, I will issue a bench warrant for your arrest on charges of malfeasance in office."

X

Colonial Marshal Max Fane was as heavy as Gus Brannhard and considerably shorter. Wedged between them on
the back seat of the marshal's car, Jack Holloway contem-
plated the backs of the two uniformed deputies on the
front seat and felt a happy smile spread through him.
Going to get his Fuzzies back. Little Fuzzy, and Ko-Ko,
and Mike, and Mamma Fuzzy, and Mitzi, and Cinderella;
he named them over and imagined them crowding around
him, happy to be back with Pappy Jack.

The car settled onto the top landing stage of the
Company's Science Center, and immediately a Company
cop came running up. Gus opened the door, and Jack
climbed out after him.

"Hey, you can't land here!" the cop was shouting. "This
is for Company executives only!"

Max Fane emerged behind them and stepped forward;
the two deputies piled out from in front.

"The hell you say, now," Fane said. "A court order
lands anywhere. Bring him along, boys; we wouldn't want
him to go and bump himself on a communication screen
anywhere."

The Company cop started to protest, then subsided and
fell in between the deputies. Maybe it was beginning to
dawn on him that the Federation courts were bigger than
the chartered Zarathustra Company after all. Or maybe
he just thought there'd been a revolution.

Leonard Kellogg's—temporarily Ernst Mallin's—office
was on the first floor of the penthouse, counting down
from the top landing stage. When they stepped from the
escalator, the hall was crowded with office people, gabbling excitedly in groups; they all stopped talking as soon
as they saw what was coming. In the division chief's outer
office three or four girls jumped to their feet; one of them
jumped into the bulk of Marshal Fane, which had inter-
posed itself between her and the communication screen.

They were all shooed out into the hall, and one of the deputies was dropped there with the prisoner. The middle office was empty. Fane took his badgeholder in his left hand as he pushed through the door to the inner office.

Kellogg's—temporarily Mallin's—secretary seemed to have preceded them by a few seconds; she was standing in front of the desk sputtering incoherently. Mallin, starting to rise from his chair, froze, hunched forward over the desk. Juan Jimenez, standing in the middle of the room, seemed to have seen them first; he was looking about wildly as though for some way of escape.

Fane pushed past the secretary and went up to the desk, showing Mallin his badge and then serving the papers. Mallin looked at him in bewilderment.

"But we're keeping those Fuzzies for Mr. O'Brien, the Chief Prosecutor," he said. "We can't turn them over without his authorization."

"This," Max Fane said gently, "is an order of the court, issued by Chief Justice Pendarvis. As for Mr. O'Brien, I doubt if he's Chief Prosecutor any more. In fact, I suspect that he's in jail. *And that*," he shouted, leaning forward as far as his waistline would permit and banging on the desk with his fist, "*is where I'm going to stuff you, if you don't get those Fuzzies in here and turn them over immediately!*"

If Fane had suddenly metamorphosed himself into a damnthing, it couldn't have shaken Mallin more. Involuntarily he cringed from the marshal, and that finished him.

"But I can't," he protested. "We don't know exactly where they are at the moment."

"You don't know." Fane's voice sank almost to a whisper. "You admit you're holding them here, but you . . . don't . . . know . . . where. *Now start over again; tell the truth this time!*"

At that moment, the communication screen began making a fuss. Ruth Ortheris, in a light blue tailored costume, appeared in it.

"Dr. Mallin, what *is* going on here?" she wanted to know. "I just came in from lunch, and a gang of men are tearing my office up. Haven't you found the Fuzzies yet?"

"What's that?" Jack yelled. At the same time, Mallin

107

was almost screaming: "Ruth! Shut up! Blank out and get out of the building!"

With surprising speed for a man of his girth, Fane whirled and was in front of the screen, holding his badge out.

"I'm Colonel Marshal Fane. Now, young woman; I want you up here right away. Don't make me send anybody after you, because I won't like that and neither will you."

"Right away, Marshal." She blanked the screen.

Fane turned to Mallin. "Now." He wasn't bothering with vocal tricks any more. "Are you going to tell me the truth, or am I going to run you in and put a veridicator on you? Where are those Fuzzies?"

"But I don't know!" Mallin wailed. "Juan, you tell him; you took charge of them. I haven't even seen them since they were brought here."

Jack managed to fight down the fright that was clutching at him and got control of his voice.

"If anything's happened to those Fuzzies, you two are going to envy Kurt Borch before I'm through with you," he said.

"All right, how about it?" Fane asked Jimenez. "Start with when you and Ham O'Brien picked up the Fuzzies at Central Courts Building last night.

"Well, we brought them here. I'd gotten some cages fixed up for them, and—"

Ruth Ortheris came in. She didn't try to avoid Jack's eyes, nor did she try to brazen it out with him. She merely nodded distantly, as though they'd met on a ship sometime, and sat down.

"What happened, Marshal?" she asked. "Why are you here with these gentlemen?"

"The court's ordered the Fuzzies returned to Mr. Holloway." Mallin was in a dither. "He has some kind a writ or something, and we don't know where they are."

"Oh, no!" Ruth's face, for an instant, was dismay itself. "Not when—" Then she froze shut.

"I came in about o-seven-hundred," Jimenez was saying, "to give them food and water, and they'd broken out of their cages. The netting was broken loose on one cage and the Fuzzy that had been in it had gotten out and let the others out. They got into my office—they made a perfect shambles of it—and got out the door into the hall, and now we don't know where they are. And I don't know how they did any of it."

Cages built for something with no hands and almost no brains. Ever since Kellogg and Mallin had come to the camp, Mallin had been hynotizing himself into the just-silly-little-animals doctrine. He must have succeeded; last night he'd acted accordingly.

"We want to see the cages," Jack said.

"Yeah." Fane went to the outer door. "Miguel."

The deputy came in, herding the Company cop ahead of him.

"You heard what happened?" Fane asked.

"Yeah. Big Fuzzy jailbreak. What did they do, make little wooden pistols and bluff their way out?"

"By God, I wouldn't put it past them. Come along. Bring Chummy along with you; he knows the inside of this place better than we do. Piet, call in. We want six more men. Tell Chang to borrow from the constabulary if he has to."

"Wait a minute," Jack said. He turned to Ruth. "What do you know about this?"

"Well, not much. I was with Dr. Mallin here when Mr. Grego—I mean, Mr. O'Brien—called to tell us that the Fuzzies were going to be kept here till the trial. We were going to fix up a room for them, but till that could be done, Juan got some cages to put them in. That was all I knew about it till o-nine-thirty, when I came in and found everything in an uproar and was told that the Fuzzies had gotten loose during the night. I knew they couldn't get out of the building, so I went to my office and lab to start overhauling some equipment we were going to need with the Fuzzies. About ten-hundred, I found that I couldn't do anything with it, and my assistant and I loaded it on a pickup truck and took it to Henry Stenson's instrument shop. By the time I was through there, I had lunch and then came back here."

He wondered briefly how a polyencephalographic veridicator would react to some of those statements; might be a good idea if Max Fane found out.

"I'll stay here," Gus Brannhard was saying, "and see if I can get some more truth out of these people."

"Why don't you screen the hotel and tell Gerd and Ben what's happened?" he asked. "Gerd used to work here; maybe he could help us hunt."

"Good idea. Piet, tell our re-enforcements to stop at the Mallory on the way and pick him up." Fane turned to Jimenez. "Come along; show us where you had these Fuzzies and how they got away."

"You say one of them broke out of his cage and then released the others," Jack said to Jimenez as they were going down on the escalator. "Do you know which one it was?"

Jimenez shook his head. "We just took them out of the bags and put them into the cages."

That would be Little Fuzzy; he'd always been the brains of the family. With his leadership, they might have a chance. The trouble was that this place was full of dangers Fuzzies knew nothing about—radiation and poisons and electric wiring and things like that. If they really had escaped. That was a possibility that began worrying Jack.

On each floor they passed going down, he could glimpse parties of Company employees in the halls, armed with nets and blankets and other catching equipment. When they got off Jimenez led them through a big room of glass cases—mounted specimens and articulated skeletons of Zarathustran mammals. More people were there, looking around and behind and even into the cases. He began to think that the escape was genuine, and not just a cover-up for the murder of the Fuzzies.

Jiminez took them down a narrow hall beyond to an open door at the end. Inside, the permanent night light made a blue-white glow; a swivel chair stood just inside the door. Jimenez pointed to it.

"They must have gotten up on that to work the latch and open the door," he said.

It was like the doors at the camp, spring latch, with a handle instead of a knob. They'd have learned how to work it from watching him. Fane was trying the latch.

"Not too stiff," he said. "Your little fellows strong enough to work it?"

He tried it and agreed. "Sure. And they'd be smart enough to do it, too. Even Baby Fuzzy, the one your men didn't get, would be able to figure that out."

"And look what they did to my office," Jimenez said, putting on the lights.

They'd made quite a mess of it. They hadn't delayed long to do it, just thrown things around. Everything was thrown off the top of the desk. They had dumped the wastebasket, and left it dumped. He saw that and chuckled. The escape had been genuine all right.

"Probably hunting for things they could use as weapons, and doing as much damage as they could in the process." There was evidently a pretty wide streak of vindictiveness in Fuzzy character. "I don't think they like you, Juan."

"Wouldn't blame them," Fane said. Let's see what kind of a houdini they did on these cages now."

The cages were in a room—file room, storeroom, junk room—behind Jimenez's office. It had a spring lock, too, and the Fuzzies had dragged one of the cages over and stood on it to open the door. The cages themselves were about three feet wide and five feet long, with plywood bottoms, wooden frames and quarter-inch netting on the sides and tops. The tops were hinged, and fastened with hasps, and bolts slipped through the staples with nuts screwed on them. The nuts had been unscrewed from five and the bolts slipped out; the sixth cage had been broken open from the inside, the netting cut away from the frame at one corner and bent back in a triangle big enough for a Fuzzy to crawl through.

"I can't understand that," Jimenez was saying. "Why that wire looks as though it had been cut."

"It was cut. Marshal, I'd pull somebody's belt about this, if I were you. Your men aren't very careful about searching prisoners. One of the Fuzzies hid a knife out on them." He remembered how Little Fuzzy and Ko-Ko had burrowed into the bedding in apparently unreasoning panic, and explained about the little spring-steel knives he had made. "I suppose he palmed it and hugged himself into a ball, as though he was scared witless, when they put him in the bag."

"Waited till he was sure he wouldn't get caught before he used it, too," the marshal said. "That wire's soft enough to cut easily." He turned to Jimenez. "You people ought to be glad I'm ineligible for jury duty. Why don't you just throw it in and let Kellogg cop a plea?"

111

Gerd von Riebeek stopped for a moment in the doorway and looked into what had been Leonard Kellogg's office. The last time he'd been here, Kellogg had had him on the carpet about that land-prawn business. Now Ernst Mallin was sitting in Kellogg's chair, trying to look unconcerned and not making a very good job of it. Gus Brannhard sprawled in an armchair, smoking a cigar and looking at Mallin as he would look at a river pig when he doubted whether it was worth shooting it or not. A uniformed deputy turned quickly, then went back to studying an elaborate wall chart showing the interrelation of Zarathustran mammals—he'd made the original of that chart himself. And Ruth Ortheris sat apart from the desk and the three men, smoking. She looked up and then, when she saw that he was looking past and away from her, she lowered her eyes.

"You haven't found them?" he asked Brannhard.

The fluffy-bearded lawyer shook his head. "Jack has a gang down in the cellar, working up. Max is in the psychology lab, putting the Company cops who were on duty last night under veridication. They all claim, and the veridicator backs them up, that it was impossible for the Fuzzies to get out of the building."

"They don't know what's impossible, for a Fuzzy."

"That's what I told him. He didn't give me any argument, either. He's pretty impressed with how they got out of those cages."

Ruth spoke. "Gerd, we didn't hurt them. We weren't going to hurt them at all. Juan put them in cages because we didn't have any other place for them, but we were going to fix up a nice room, where they could play together. . . ." Then she must have seen that he wasn't listening, and stopped, crushing out her cigarette and rising. "Dr. Mallin, if these people haven't any more questions to ask me, I have a lot of work to do."

"You want to ask her anything, Gerd?" Brannhard inquired.

Once he had had something very important he had wanted to ask her. He was glad, now, that he hadn't gotten around to it. Hell, she was so married to the Company it'd be bigamy if she married him too.

"No. I don't want to talk to her at all."

She started for the door, then hesitated. "Gerd, I . . ." she began. Then she went out. Gus Brannhard looked after her, and dropped the ash of his cigar on Leonard Kellogg's—now Ernst Mallin's—floor.

Gerd detested her, and she wouldn't have had any respect for him if he didn't. She ought to have known that something like this would happen. It always did, in the business. A smart girl, in the business, never got involved with any one man; she always got herself four or five boyfriends, on all possible sides, and played them off one against another.

She'd have to get out of the Science Center right away. Marshal Fane was questioning people under verification; she didn't dare let him get around to her. She didn't dare go to her office; the veridicator was in the lab across the hall, and that's where he was working. And she didn't dare—

Yes, she could do that, by screen. She went into an office down the hall; a dozen people recognized her at once and began bombarding her with questions about the Fuzzies. She brushed them off and went to a screen, punching a combination. After a slight delay, an elderly man with a thin-lipped, bloodless face appeared. When he recognized her, there was a brief look of annoyance on the thin face.

"Mr. Stenson," she began, before he could say anything. "That apparatus I brought to your shop this morning— the sensory-response detector—we've made a simply frightful mistake. There's nothing wrong with it whatever, and if anything's done with it, it may cause serious damage."

"I don't think I understand, Dr. Ortheris."

"Well, it was a perfectly natural mistake. You see, we're all at our wits' end here. Mr. Holloway and his lawyer and the Colonial Marshal are here with an order from Judge Pendarvis for the return of those Fuzzies. None of us know what we're doing at all. Why the whole trouble with the apparatus was the fault of the operator. We'll have to have it back immediately, all of it."

"I see, Dr. Ortheris." The old instrument maker looked worried. "But I'm afraid the apparatus has already gone to the workroom. Mr. Stephenson has it now, and I can't get in touch with him at present. If the mistake can be corrected, what do you want done?"

"Just hold it; I'll call or send for it."

She blanked the screen. Old Johnson, the chief data synthesist, tried to detain her with some question.

"I'm sorry, Mr. Johnson. I can't stop now. I have to go over to Company House right away."

The suite at the Hotel Mallory was crowded when Jack Holloway returned with Gerd van Riebeek; it was noisy with voices, and the ventilators were laboring to get rid of the tobacco smoke. Gus Brannhard, Ben Rainsford and Baby Fuzzy were meeting the press.

"Oh, Mr. Holloway!" somebody shouted as he entered. "Have you found them yet?"

"No; we've been all over Science Center from top to bottom. We know they went down a few floors from where they'd been caged, but that's all. I don't think they could have gotten outside; the only exit on the ground level's through a vestibule where a Company policeman was on duty, and there's no way for them to have climbed down from any of the terraces or landing stages."

"Well, Mr. Holloway, I hate to suggest this," somebody else said, "but have you eliminated the possibility that they may have hidden in a trash bin and been dumped into the mass-energy converter?"

"We thought of that. The converter's underground, in a vault that can be entered only by one door, and that was locked. No trash was disposed of between the time they were brought there and the time the search started, and everything that's been sent to the converter since has been checked piece by piece."

"Well, I'm glad to hear that, Mr. Holloway, and I know that everybody hearing this will be glad, too. I take it you've not given up looking for them?"

"Are we on the air now? No, I have not; I'm staying here in Mallorysport until I either find them or am convinced that they aren't in the city. And I am offering a reward of two thousand sols apiece for their return to me. If you'll wait a moment, I'll have descriptions ready for you. . . ."

Victor Gregg unstoppered the refrigerated cocktail jug. "More?" he asked Leslie Coombes.

"Yes, thank you." Coombes held his glass until it was filled. "As you say, Victor, you made the decision, but you made it on my advice, and the advice was bad."

He couldn't disagree, even politely, with that. He hoped it hadn't been ruinously bad. One thing, Leslie wasn't trying to pass the buck, and considering how Ham O'Brien had mishandled his end of it, he could have done so quite plausibly.

"I used bad judgment," Coombes said dispassionately, as though discussing some mistake Hitler had made, or Napoleon. "I thought O'Brien wouldn't try to use one of those presigned writs, and I didn't think Pendarvis would admit, publicly, that he signed court orders in blank. He's been severely criticized by the press about that."

He hadn't thought Brannhard and Holloway would try to fight a court order either. That was one of the consequences of being too long in a seemingly irresistible position; you didn't expect resistance. Kellogg hadn't expected Jack Holloway to order him off his land grant. Kurt Borch had thought all he needed to do with a gun was pull it and wave it around. And Jimenez had expected the Fuzzies to just sit in their cages.

"I wonder where they got to," Coombes was saying. "I understand they couldn't be found at all in the building."

"Ruth Ortheris has an idea. She got away from Science Center before Fane could get hold of her and veridicate her. It seems she and an assistant took some apparatus out, about ten o'clock, in a truck. She thinks the Fuzzies hitched a ride with her. I know that sounds rather improbable, but hell, everything else sounds impossible. I'll have it followed up. Maybe we can find them before Holloway does. They're not inside Science Center, that's sure." His own glass was empty; he debated a refill and voted against it. "O'Brien's definitely out, I take it?"

"Completely. Pendarvis gave him his choice of resigning or facing malfeasance charges."

"They couldn't really convict him of malfeasance for that, could they? Malfeasance, maybe, but—"

"They could charge him. And then they could interro-

115

gate him under veridication about his whole conduct in office, and you know what they would bring out," Coombes said. "He almost broke an arm signing his resignation. He's still Attorney General of the Colony, of course; Nick issued a statement supporting him. That hasn't done Nick as much harm as O'Brien could do spilling what he knows about Residency affairs.

"Now Brannhard is talking about bringing suit against the Company, and he's furnishing copies of all the Fuzzy films Holloway has to the news services. Interworld News is going hog-wild with it, and even the services we control can't play it down too much. I don't know who's going to be prosecuting these cases, but whoever it is, he won't dare pull any punches. And the whole thing's made Pendarvis hostile to us. I know, the law and the evidence and nothing but the law and the evidence, but the evidence is going to filter into his conscious mind through this hostility. He's called a conference with Brannhard and myself for tomorrow afternoon; I don't know what that's going to be like."

XI

The two lawyers had risen hastily when Chief Justice Pendarvis entered; he responded to their greetings and seated himself at his desk, reaching for the silver cigar box and taking out a panatella. Gustavus Adolphus Brannhard picked up the cigar he had laid aside and began puffing on it; Leslie Coombes took a cigarette from his case. They both looked at him, waiting like two drawn weapons—a battle ax and a rapier.

"Well, gentlemen, as you know, we have a couple of homicide cases and nobody to prosecute them," he began.

"Why bother, your Honor?" Coombes asked. "Both charges are completely frivolous. One man killed a wild animal, and the other killed a man who was trying to kill him."

"Well, your Honor, I don't believe my client is guilty of anything, legally or morally," Brannhard said. "I want that established by an acquittal." He looked at Coombes. "I should think Mr. Coombes would be just as anxious to have his client cleared of any stigma of murder, too."

"I am quite agreed. People who have been charged with crimes ought to have public vindication if they are innocent. Now, in the first place, I planned to hold the Kellogg trial first, and then the Holloway trial. Are you both satisfied with that arrangement?"

"Absolutely not, your Honor," Brannhard said promptly. "The whole basis of the Holloway defense is that this man Borch was killed in commission of a felony. We're prepared to prove that, but we don't want our case prejudiced by an earlier trial."

Coombes laughed. "Mr. Brannhard wants to clear his client by preconvicting mine. We can't agree to anything like that."

"Yes, and he is making the same objection to trying your client first. Well, I'm going to remove both objections. I'm going to order the two cases combined, and both defendants tried together."

A momentary glow of unholy glee on Gus Brannhard's face; Coombes didn't like the idea at all.

"Your Honor, I trust that that suggestion was only made facetiously," he said.

"It wasn't, Mr. Coombes."

"Then if your Honor will not hold me in contempt for saying so, it is the most shockingly irregular—I won't go so far as to say improper—trial procedure I've ever heard of. This is not a case of accomplices charged with the same crime; this is a case of two men charged with different criminal acts, and the conviction of either would mean the almost automatic acquittal of the other. I don't know who's going to be named to take Mohammed O'Brien's place, but I pity him from the bottom of my heart. Why, Mr. Brannhard and I could go off somewhere and play poker while the prosecutor would smash the case to pieces."

"Well, we won't have just one prosecutor, Mr. Coombes, we will have two. I'll swear you and Mr. Brannhard in as special prosecutors, and you can prosecute Mr. Brannhard's client, and he yours. I think that would remove any further objections."

It was all he could do to keep his face judicially grave and unmirthful. Brannhard was almost purring, like a big tiger that had just gotten the better of a young goat; Leslie Coombes's suavity was beginning to crumble slightly at the edges.

"Your Honor, that is a most excellent suggestion," Brannhard declared. "I will prosecute Mr. Coombes's client with the greatest pleasure in the universe."

"Well, all I can say, your Honor, is that if the first proposal was the most irregular I had ever heard, the record didn't last long!"

"Why, Mr. Coombes, I went over the law and the rules of jurisprudence very carefully, and I couldn't find a word that could be construed as disallowing such a procedure."

"I'll bet you didn't find any precedent for it either!"

Leslie Coombes should have known better than that; in colonial law, you can find a precedent for almost anything.

"How much do you bet, Leslie?" Brannhard asked, a larcenous gleam in his eye.

"Don't let him take your money away from you. I

found, inside an hour, sixteen precedents, from twelve different planetary jurisdictions."

"All right, your Honor," Coombes capitulated. "But I hope you know what you're doing. You're turning a couple of cases of the People of the Colony into a common civil lawsuit."

Gus Brannhard laughed. "What else is it?" he demanded. "*Friends of Little Fuzzy* versus *The chartered Zarathustra Company;* I'm bringing action as friend of incompetent aborigines for recognition of sapience, and Mr. Coombes, on behalf of the Zarathustra Company, is contesting to preserve the Company's charter, and that's all there is or ever was to this case."

That was impolite of Gus. Leslie Coombes had wanted to go on to the end pretending that the Company charter had absolutely nothing to do with it.

There was an unending stream of reports of Fuzzies seen here and there, often simultaneously in impossibly distant parts of the city. Some were from publicity seekers and pathological liars and crackpots; some were the result of honest mistakes or overimaginativeness. There was some reason to suspect that not a few had originated with the Company, to confuse the search. One thing did come to light which heartened Jack Holloway. An intensive if concealed search was being made by the Company police, and by the Mallorysport police department, which the Company controlled.

Max Fane was giving every available moment to the hunt. This wasn't because of ill will for the Company, though that was present, nor because the Chief Justice was riding him. The Colonial Marshal was pro-Fuzzy. So were the Colonial Constabulary, over whom Nick Emmert's administration seemed to have little if any authority. Colonel Ian Ferguson, the commandant, had his appointment direct from the Colonial Office on Terra. He had called by screen to offer his help, and George Lunt, over on Beta, screened daily to learn what progress was being made.

Living at the Hotel Mallory was expensive, and Jack had to sell some sunstones. The Company gem buyers were barely civil to him; he didn't try to be civil at all. There was also a noticeable coolness toward him at the bank. On the other hand, on several occasions, Space Navy officers and ratings down from Xerxes Base went out of their way to accost him, introduce themselves, shake hands with him and give him their best wishes.

Once, in one of the weather-domed business centers, an elderly man with white hair showing under his black beret greeted him.

"Mr. Holloway, I want to tell you how grieved I am to learn about the disappearance of those little people of yours," he said. "I'm afraid there's nothing I can do to help you, but I hope they turn up safely."

"Why, thank you, Mr. Stenson." He shook hands with the old master instrument maker. "If you could make me a pocket veridicator, to use on some of these people who claim they saw them, it would be a big help."

"Well, I do make rather small portable veridicators for the constabulary, but I think what you need is an instrument for detection of psychopaths, and that's slightly beyond science at present. But if you're still prospecting for sunstones, I have an improved microray scanner I just developed, and . . ."

He walked with Stenson to his shop, had a cup of tea and looked at the scanner. From Stenson's screen, he called Max Fane. Six more people had claimed to have seen the Fuzzies.

Within a week, the films taken at the camp had been shown so frequently on telecast as to wear out their interest value. Baby, however, was still available for new pictures, and in a few days a girl had to be hired to take care of his fan mail. Once, entering a bar, Jack thought he saw Baby sitting on a woman's head. A second look showed that it was only a life-sized doll, held on with an elastic band. Within a week, he was seeing Baby Fuzzy hats all over town, and shop windows were full of life-sized Fuzzy dolls.

In the late afternoon, two weeks after the Fuzzies had vanished, Marshal Fane dropped him at the hotel. They sat in the car for a moment, and Fane said:

"I think this is the end of it. We're all out of cranks and exhibitionists now."

He nodded. "That woman we were talking to. She's crazy as a bedbug."

"Yeah. In the past ten years she's confessed to every un-solved crime on the planet. It shows you how hard up we are that I waste your time and mine listening to her."

"Max, nobody's seen them. You think they just aren't, any more, don't you?"

The fat man looked troubled. "Well, Jack, it isn't so much that nobody's seen them. Nobody's seen any trace of them. There are land-prawns all around, but nobody's found a cracked shell. And six active, playful, inquisitive Fuzzies ought to be getting into things. They ought to be raiding food markets, and fruit stands, getting into places and ransacking. But there hasn't been a thing. The Company police have stopped looking for them now."

"Well, I won't. They must be around somewhere." He shook Fane's hand, and got out of the car. "You've been awfully helpful, Max. I want you to know how much I thank you."

He watched the car lift away, and then looked out over the city—a vista of treetop green, with roofs and the domes of shopping centers and business centers and amusement centers showing through, and the angular buttes of tall buildings rising above. The streetless contra-gravity city of a new planet that had never known ground traffic. The Fuzzies could be hiding anywhere among those trees—or they could all be dead in some man-made trap. He thought of all the deadly places into which they could have wandered. Machinery, dormant and quiet, until somebody threw a switch. Conduits, which could be flood-ed without warning, or filled with scalding steam or chok-ing gas. Poor little Fuzzies, they'd think a city was as safe as the woods of home, where there was nothing worse than harpies and damnthings.

Gus Brannhard was out when he went down to the suite; Ben Rainsford was at a reading screen, studying a psychology text, and Gerd was working at a desk that had been brought in. Baby was playing on the floor with the bright new toys they had gotten for him. When Pappy Jack came in, he dropped them and ran to be picked up and held.

"George called," Gerd said. "They have a family of Fuzzies at the post now."

"Well, that's great." He tried to make it sound enthusiastic. "How many?"

"Five, three males and two females. They call them Dr. Crippen, Dillinger, Ned Kelly, Lizzie Borden and Calamity Jane."

Wouldn't it be just like a bunch of cops to hang names like that on innocent Fuzzies?

"Why don't you call the post and say hello to them?" Ben asked.

"Baby likes them; he'd think it was fun to talk to them again."

He let himself be urged into it, and punched out the combination. They were nice Fuzzies; almost, but of course not quite, as nice as his own.

"If your family doesn't turn up in time for the trial, have Gus subpoena ours," Lunt told him. "You ought to have some to produce in court. Two weeks from now, this mob of ours will be doing all kinds of things. You ought to see them now, and we only got them yesterday afternoon."

He said he hoped he'd have his own by then; he realized that he was saying it without much conviction.

They had a drink when Gus came in. He was delighted with the offer from Lunt. Another one who didn't expect to see Pappy Jack's Fuzzies alive again.

"I'm not doing a damn thing here," Rainsford said. "I'm going back to Beta till the trial. Maybe I can pick up some ideas from George Lunt's Fuzzies. I'm damned if I'm getting any from this crap!" He gestured at the reading screen. "All I have is a vocabulary, and I don't know what half the words mean." He snapped it off. "I'm beginning to wonder if maybe Jimenez mightn't have been right and Ruth Ortheris is wrong. Maybe you can be just a little bit sapient."

"Maybe it's possible to be sapient and not know it," Gus said. "Like the character in the old French play who didn't know he was talking prose."

"What do you mean, Gus?" Gerd asked.

"I'm not sure I know. It's just an idea that occurred to me today. Kick it around and see if you can get anything out of it."

"I believe the difference lies in the area of consciousness," Ernst Mallin was saying. "You all know, of course, the axiom that only one-tenth, never more than one-eighth, of our mental activity occurs above the level of consciousness. Now let us imagine a hypothetical race whose entire mentation is conscious."

"I hope they stay hypothetical," Victor Grego, in his office across the city, said out of the screen. "They wouldn't recognize us as sapient at all."

'We wouldn't be sapient, as they'd define the term," Leslie Coombes, in the same screen with Grego, said. "They'd have some equivalent of the talk-and-build-a-fire rule, based on abilities of which we can't even conceive."

Maybe, Ruth thought, they might recognize us as one-tenth to as much as one-eighth sapient. No, then we'd have to recognize, say, a chimpanzee as being one-one-hundredth sapient, and a flatworm as being sapient to the order of one-billionth.

"Wait a minute," she said. "If I understand, you mean that nonsapient beings think, but only subconsciously?"

"That's correct, Ruth. When confronted by some entirely novel situation, a nonsapient animal will think, but never consciously. Of course, familiar situations are dealt with by pure habit and memory-response."

"You know, I've just thought of something," Grego said. "I think we can explain that funeral that's been bothering all of us in nonsapient terms." He lit a cigarette, while they all looked at him expectantly. "Fuzzies," he continued, "bury their ordure: they do this to avoid an unpleasant sense-stimulus, a bad smell. Dead bodies quickly putrefy and smell badly; they are thus equated, subconsciously, with ordure and must be buried. All Fuzzies carry weapons. A Fuzzy's weapon is—still subconsciously—regarded as a part of the Fuzzy, hence it must also be buried."

Mallin frowned portentiously. The idea seemed to appeal to him, but of course he simply couldn't agree too promptly with a mere layman, even the boss.

"Well, so far you're on fairly safe ground, Mr. Grego," he admitted. "Association of otherwise dissimilar things because of some apparent similarity is a recognized element of nonsapient animal behavior." He frowned again. "That *could* be an explanation. I'll have to think of it."

About this time tomorrow, it would be his own idea,

with grudging recognition of a suggestion by Victor Grego. In time, that would be forgotten; it would be the Mallin Theory. Grego was apparently agreeable, as long as the job got done.

"Well, if you can make anything out of it, pass it on to Mr. Coombes as soon as possible, to be worked up for use in court," he said.

XII

Ben Rainsford went back to Beta Continent, and Gerd van Riebeek remained in Mallorysport. The constabulary at Post Fifteen had made steel chopper-diggers for their Fuzzies, and reported a gratifying abatement of the land-prawn nuisance. They also made a set of scaled-down carpenter tools, and their Fuzzies were building themselves a house out of scrap crates and boxes. A pair of Fuzzies showed up at Ben Rainsford's camp, and he adopted them, naming them Flora and Fauna.

Everybody had Fuzzies now, and Pappy Jack only had Baby. He was lying on the floor of the parlor, teaching Baby to tie knots in a piece of string. Gus Brannhard, who spent most of the day in the office in the Central Courts building which had been furnished to him as special prosecutor, was lolling in an armchair in red-and-blue pajamas, smoking a cigar, drinking coffee—his whisky consumption was down to a couple of drinks a day—and studying texts on two reading screens at once, making an occasional remark into a stenomemophone. Gerd was at the desk, spoiling notepaper in an effort to work something out by symbolic logic. Suddenly he crumpled a sheet and threw it across the room, cursing. Brannhard looked away from his screens.

"Trouble, Gerd?"

Gerd cursed again. "How the devil can I tell whether Fuzzies generalize?" he demanded. "How can I tell whether they form abstract ideas? How can I prove, even, that they have ideas at all? Hell's blazes, how can I even prove, to your satisfaction, that I think consciously?"

"Working on that idea I mentioned?" Brannhard asked.

"I was. It seemed like a good idea but . . ."

"Suppose we go back to specific instances of Fuzzy behavior, and present them as evidence of sapience?" Brannhard asked. "That funeral, for instance."

"They'll still insist that we define sapience."

The communication screen began buzzing. Baby Fuzzy looked up disinterestedly, and then went back to trying to untie a figure-eight knot he had tied. Jack shoved himself to his feet and put the screen on. It was Max Fane, and for the first time that he could remember, the Colonial Marshal was excited.

"Jack, have you had any news on the screen lately?"

"No. Something turn up?"

"God, yes! The cops are all over the city hunting the Fuzzies; they have orders to shoot on sight. Nick Emmert was just on the air with a reward offer—five hundred sols apiece, dead or alive."

It took a few seconds for that to register. Then he became frightened. Gus and Gerd were both on their feet and crowding to the screen behind him.

"They have some bum from that squatters' camp over on the East Side who claims the Fuzzies beat up his ten-year-old daughter," Fane was saying. "They have both of them at police headquarters, and they've handed the story out to Zarathustra News, and Planetwide Coverage. Of course, they're Company-controlled; they're playing it for all it's worth."

"Have they been veridicated?" Brannhard demanded.

"No, and the city cops are keeping them under cover. The girl says she was playing outdoors and these Fuzzies jumped her and began beating her with sticks. Her injuries are listed as multiple bruises, fractured wrist and general shock."

"I don't believe it! They wouldn't attack a child."

"I want to talk to that girl and her father," Brannhard was saying. "And I'm going to demand that they make their statements under veridication. This thing's a frame-up, Max; I'd bet my ears on it. Timing's just right; only a week till the trial."

Maybe the Fuzzies had wanted the child to play with them, and she'd gotten frightened and hurt one of them. A ten-year-old human child would look dangerously large to a Fuzzy, and if they thought they were menaced they would fight back savagely.

They were still alive and in the city. That was one thing. But they were in worse danger than they had ever

126

been; that was another. Fane was asking Brannhard how soon he could be dressed.

"Five minutes? Good, I'll be along to pick you up," he said. "Be seeing you."

Jack hurried into the bedroom he and Brannhard shared; he kicked off his moccasins and began pulling on his boots. Brannhard, pulling his trousers up over his pajama pants, wanted to know where he thought he was going.

"With you. I've got to find them before some dumb son of a Khooghra shoots them."

"You stay here," Gus ordered. "Stay by the communication screen, and keep the viewscreen on for news. But don't stop putting your boots on; you may have to get out of here fast if I call you and tell you they've been located. I'll call you as soon as I get anything definite."

Gerd had the screen on for news, and was getting Planetwide, openly owned and operated by the Company. The newscaster was wrought up about the brutal attack on the innocent child, but he was having trouble focusing the blame. After all, who'd let the Fuzzies escape in the first place? And even a skilled semanticist had trouble in making anything called a Fuzzy sound menacing. At least he gave particulars, true or not.

The child, Lolita Lurkin, had been playing outside her home at about twenty-one hundred when she had suddenly been set upon by six Fuzzies, armed with clubs. Without provocation, they had dragged her down and beaten her severely. Her screams had brought her father, and he had driven the Fuzzies away. Police had brought both the girl and her father, Oscar Lurkin, to headquarters, where they had told their story. City police, Company police and constabulary troopers and parties of armed citizens were combing the eastern side of the city; Resident General Emmert had acted at once to offer a reward of five thousand sols apiece. . . .

"The kid's lying, and if they ever get a veridicator on her, they'll prove it," he said. "Emmert, or Grego, or the two of them together, bribed those people to tell that story."

"Oh, I take that for granted," Gerd said. "I know that place. Junktown. Ruth does a lot of work there for juvenile court." He stopped briefly, pain in his eyes, and then continued: "You can hire anybody to do anything over there for a hundred sols, especially if the cops are fixed in advance."

He shifted to the Interworld News frequency; they were covering the Fuzzy hunt from an aircar. The shanties and parked airjalopies of Junktown were floodlighted from above; lines of men were beating the brush and poking among them. Once a car passed directly below the pickup, a man staring at the ground from it over a machine gun.

"Wooo! Am I glad I'm not in that mess!" Gerd exclaimed. "Anybody sees something he thinks is a Fuzzy and half that gang'll massacre each other in ten seconds."

"I hope they do!"

Interworld News was pro-Fuzzy; the commentator in the car was being extremely saracastic about the whole thing. Into the middle of one view of a rifle-bristling line of beaters somebody in the studio cut a view of the Fuzzies, taken at the camp, looking up appealingly while waiting for breakfast. "These," a voice said, "are the terrible monsters against whom all these brave men are protecting us."

A few moments later, a rifle flash and a bang, and then a fusillade brought Jack's heart into his throat. The pickup car jetted toward it; by the time it reached the spot, the shooting had stopped, and a crowd was gathering around something white on the ground. He had to force himself to look, then gave a shuddering breath of relief. It was a zaragoat, a three-horned domesticated ungulate.

"Oh-Oh! Some squatter's milk supply finished." The commentator laughed. "Not the first one tonight either. Attorney General—former Chief Prosecutor—O'Brien's going to have quite a few suits against the administration to defend as a result of this business."

"He's going to have a goddamn thundering big one from Jack Holloway!"

The communication screen buzzed; Gerd snapped it on.

"I just talked to Judge Pendarvis," Gus Brannhard reported out of it. "He's issuing an order restraining Emmert from paying any reward except for Fuzzies turned over alive and uninjured to Marshal Fane. And he's issuing a warning that until the status of the Fuzzies is determined, anybody killing one will face charges of murder."

"That's fine, Gus! Have you seen the girl or her father yet?"

Brannhard snarled angrily. "The girl's in the Company hospital, in a private room. The doctors won't let anybody see her. I think Emmert's hiding the father in the Residency. And I haven't seen the two cops who brought them in, or the desk sergeant who booked the complaint, or the detective lieutenant who was on duty here. They've all lammed out. Max has a couple of men over in Junktown, trying to find out who called the cops in the first place. We may get something out of that."

The Chief Justice's action was announced a few minutes later; it got to the hunters a few minutes after that and the Fuzzy hunt began falling apart. The City and Company police dropped out immediately. Most of the civilians, hoping to grab five thousand sols' worth of live Fuzzy, stayed on for twenty minutes, and so, apparently to control them, did the constabulary. Then the reward was cancelled, the airborne floodlights went off and the whole thing broke up.

Gus Brannhard came in shortly afterward, starting to undress as soon as he heeled the door shut after him. When he had his jacket and neckcloth off, he dropped into a chair, filled a water tumbler with whisky, gulped half of it and then began pulling off his boots.

"If that drink has a kid sister, I'll take it," Gerd muttered. "What happened, Gus?"

Brannhard began to curse. "The whole thing's a fake; it stinks from here to Nifflheim. It would stink on Nifflheim." He picked up a cigar butt he had laid aside when Fane's call had come in and relighted it. "We found the woman who called the police. Neighbor; she says she saw Lurkin come home drunk, and a little later she heard the girl screaming. She says he beats her up every time he gets drunk, which is about five times a week, and she'd made up her mind to stop it the next chance she got. She denied having seen anything that even looked like a Fuzzy anywhere around."

The excitement of the night before had incubated a new brood of Fuzzy reports; Jack went to the marshal's office to interview the people making them. The first dozen were of a piece with the ones that had come in originally.

129

Then he talked to a young man who had something of different quality.

"I saw them as plain as I'm seeing you, not more than fifty feet away," he said. "I had an autocarbine, and I pulled up on them, but, gosh, I couldn't shoot them. They were just like little people, Mr. Holloway, and they looked so scared and helpless. So I held over their heads and let off a two-second burst to scare them away before anybody else saw them and shot them."

"Well, son, I'd like to shake your hand for that. You know, you thought you were throwing away a lot of money there. How many did you see?"

"Well, only four. I'd heard that there were six, but the other two could have been back in the brush where I didn't see them."

He pointed out on the map where it had happened. There were three other people who had actually seen Fuzzies; none were sure how many, but they were all positive about locations and times. Plotting the reports on the map, it was apparent that the Fuzzies were moving north and west across the outskirts of the city.

Brannhard showed up for lunch at the hotel, still swearing, but half amusedly.

"They've exhumed Ham O'Brien, and they've put him to work harassing us," he said. "Whole flock of civil suits and dangerous-nuisance complaints and that sort of thing; idea's to keep me amused with them while Leslie Coombes is working up his case for the trial. Even tried to get the manager here to evict Baby; I threatened him with a racial-discrimination suit, and that stopped that. And I just filed suit against the Company for seven million sols on behalf of the Fuzzies—million apiece for them and a million for their lawyer."

"This evening," Jack said, "I'm going out in a car with a couple of Max's deputies. We're going to take Baby, and we'll have a loud-speaker on the car." He unfolded the city map. "They seem to be traveling this way; they ought to be about here, and with Baby at the speaker, we ought to attract their attention."

They didn't see anything, though they kept at it till dusk. Baby had a wonderful time with the loud-speaker; when he yeeked into it, he produced an ear-splitting noise, until the three humans in the car flinched every time he opened his mouth. It affected dogs too; as the car moved back and forth, it was followed by a chorus of howling and baying on the ground.

The next day, there were some scattered reports, mostly of small thefts. A blanket spread on the grass behind a house had vanished. A couple of cushions had been taken from a porch couch. A frenzied mother reported having found her six-year-old son playing with some Fuzzies; when she had rushed to rescue him, the Fuzzies had scampered away and the child had begun weeping. Jack and Gerd rushed to the scene. The child's story, jumbled and imagination-colored, was definite on one point—the Fuzzies had been nice to him and hadn't hurt him. They got a recording of that on the air at once.

When they got back to the hotel, Gus Brannhard was there, bubbling with glee.

"The Chief Justice gave me another job of special prosecuting," he said. "I'm to conduct an investigation into the possibility that this thing, the other night, was a frame-up, and I'm to prepare complaints against anybody who's done anything prosecutable. I have authority to hold hearings, and subpoena witnesses, and interrogate them under verification. Max Fane has specific orders to cooperate. We're going to start, tomorrow, with Chief of Police Dumont and work down. And maybe we can work up, too, as far as Nick Emmert and Victor Grego." He gave a rumbling laugh. "Maybe that'll give Leslie Coombes something to worry about."

Gerd brought the car down beside the rectangular excavation. It was fifty feet square and twenty feet deep, and still going deeper, with a power shovel in it and a couple of dump scows beside. Five or six men in coveralls and ankle boots advanced to meet them as they got out.

"Good morning, Mr. Holloway," one of them said. "It's right down over the edge of the hill. We haven't disturbed anything."

"Mind running over what you saw again? My partner here wasn't in when you called."

The foreman turned to Gerd. "We put off a couple of shots about an hour ago. Some of the men, who'd gone down over the edge of the hill, saw these Fuzzies run out from under that rock ledge down there, and up the hollow, that way." He pointed. "They called me, and I went down for a look, and saw where they'd been camping. The rock's pretty hard here, and we used pretty heavy charges. Shock waves in the ground was what scared them."

They started down a path through the flower-dappled tall grass toward the edge of the hill, and down past the gray outcropping of limestone that formed a miniature bluff twenty feet high and a hundred in length. Under an overhanging ledge, they found two cushions, a red-and-gray blanket, and some odds and ends of old garments that looked as though they had once been used for polishing rags. There was a broken kitchen spoon, and a cold chisel, and some other metal articles.

"That's it, all right. I talked to the people who lost the blanket and the cushions. They must have made camp last night, after your gang stopped work; the blasting chased them out. You say you saw them go up that way?" he asked, pointing up the little stream that came down from the mountains to the north.

The stream was deep and rapid, too much so for easy fording by Fuzzies; they'd follow it back into the foothills. He took everybody's names and thanked them. If he found the Fuzzies himself and had to pay off on an information-received basis, it would take a mathematical genius to decide how much reward to pay whom.

"Gerd, if you were a Fuzzy, where would you go up there?" he asked.

Gerd looked up the stream that came rushing down from among the wooded foothills.

"There are a couple more houses farther up," he said. "I'd get above them. Then I'd go up one of those side ravines, and get up among the rocks, where the damnthings couldn't get me. Of course, there are no damnthings this close to town, but they wouldn't know that."

"We'll need a few more cars. I'll call Colonel Ferguson and see what he can do for me. Max is going to have his hands full with this investigation Gus started."

Piet Dumont, the Mallorysport chief of police, might

132

have been a good cop once, but for as long as Gus Brannhard had known him, he had been what he was now—an empty shell of unsupported arrogance, with a sagging waistline and a puffy face that tried to look tough and only succeeded in looking unpleasant. He was sitting in a seat that looked like an old fashioned electric chair, or like one of those instruments of torture to which beauty-shop customers submit themselves. There was a bright conical helmet on his head, and electrodes had been clamped to various portions of his anatomy. On the wall behind him was a circular screen which ought to have been a calm turquoise blue, but which was flickering from dark blue through violet to mauve. That was simple nervous tension and guilt and anger at the humiliation of being subjected to veridicated interrogation. Now and then there would be a stabbing flicker of bright red as he toyed mentally with some deliberate misstatement of fact.

"You know, yourself, that the Fuzzies didn't hurt that girl," Brannhard told him.

"I don't know anything of the kind," the police chief retorted. "All I know's what was reported to me."

That had started out a bright red; gradually it faded into purple. Evidently Piet Dumont was adopting a rules-of-evidence definition of truth.

"Who told you about it?"

"Luther Woller. Detective lieutenant on duty at the time."

The veridicator agreed that that was the truth and not much of anything but the truth.

"But you know that what really happened was that Lurkin beat the girl himself, and Woller persuaded them both to say the Fuzzies did it," Max Fane said.

"I don't know anything of the kind!" Dumont almost yelled. The screen blazed red. "All I know's what they told me; nobody said anything else. Red and blue, juggling in a typical quibbling pattern. "As far as I know, it was the Fuzzies done it."

"Now, Piet," Fane told him patiently. "You've used this same veridicator here often enough to know you can't get away with lying on it. Woller's making you the patsy for this, and you know that, too. Isn't it true, now, that to the best of your knowledge and belief those Fuzzies never

133

touched that girl, and it wasn't till Woller talked to Lurkin and his daughter at headquarters that anybody even mentioned Fuzzies?"

The screen darkened to midnight blue, and then, slowly, it lightened.

"Yeah, that's true," Dumont admitted. He avoided their eyes, and his voice was surly. "I thought that was how it was, and I asked Woller. He just laughed at me and told me to forget it." The screen seethed momentarily with anger. "That son of a Khooghra thinks he's chief, not me. One word from me and he does just what he damn pleases!"

"Now you're being smart, Piet," Fane said. "Let's start all over. . . ."

A constabulary corporal was at the controls of the car Jack had rented from the hotel: Gerd had taken his place in one of the two constabulary cars. The third car shuttled between them, and all three talked back and forth by radio.

"Mr. Holloway." It was the trooper in the car Gerd had been piloting. "Your partner's down on the ground; he just called me with his portable. He's found a cracked prawn-shell."

"Keep talking; give me direction," the corporal at the controls said, lifting up.

In a moment, they sighted the other car, hovering over a narrow ravine on the left bank of the stream. The third car was coming in from the north. Gerd was still squatting on the ground when they let down beside him. He looked up as they jumped out.

"This is it, Jack," he said. "Regular Fuzzy job."

So it was. Whatever they had used, it hadn't been anything sharp; the head was smashed instead of being cleanly severed. The shell, however, had been broken from underneath in the standard manner, and all four mandibles had been broken off for picks. They must have all eaten at the prawn, share alike. It had been done quite recently.

They sent the car up, and while all three of them circled about, they went up the ravine on foot, calling: "Little Fuzzy! Little Fuzzy!" They found a footprint, and then another, where seepage water had moistened the ground. Gerd was talking excitedly into the portable radio he carried slung on his chest.

"One of you, go ahead a quarter of a mile, and then circle back. They're in here somewhere."

"I see them! I see them!" a voice whooped out of the radio. "They're going up the slope on your right, among the rocks!"

"Keep them in sight; somebody come and pick us up, and we'll get above them and head them off."

The rental car dropped quickly, the corporal getting the door open. He didn't bother going off contragravity; as soon as they were in and had pulled the door shut behind them, he was lifting again. For a moment, the hill sung giddily as the car turned, and then Jack saw them, climbing the steep slope among the rocks. Only four of them, and one was helping another. He wondered which ones they were, what had happened to the other two and if the one that needed help had been badly hurt.

The car landed on the top, among the rocks, settling at an awkward angle. He, Gerd and the pilot piled out and started climbing and sliding down the declivity. Then he found himself within reach of a Fuzzy and grabbed. Two more dashed past him, up the steep hill. The one he snatched at had something in his hand, and aimed a vicious blow at his face with it; he had barely time to block it with his forearm. Then he was clutching the Fuzzy and disarming him; the weapon was a quarter-pound ball-peen hammer. He put it in his hip pocket and then picked up the struggling Fuzzy with both hands.

"You hit Pappy Jack!" he said reproachfully. "Don't you know Pappy any more? Poor scared little thing!"

The Fuzzy in his arms yeeked angrily. Then he looked, and it was no Fuzzy he had ever seen before—not Little Fuzzy, nor funny, pompous Ko-Ko, nor mischievous Mike. It was a stranger Fuzzy.

"Well, no wonder; of course you didn't know Pappy Jack. You aren't one of Pappy Jack's Fuzzies at all!"

At the top, the constabulary corporal was sitting on a rock, clutching two Fuzzies, one under each arm. They stopped struggling and yeeked piteously when they saw their companion also a captive.

"Your partner's down below, chasing the other one,"

the corporal said. "You better take these too; you know them and I don't."

"Hang onto them; they don't know me any better than they do you."

With one hand, he got a bit of Extee Three out of his coat and offered it; the Fuzzy gave a cry of surprised pleasure, snatched it and gobbled it. He must have eaten it before. When he gave some to the corporal, the other two, a male and a female, also seemed familiar with it. From below, Gerd was calling:

"I got one. It's a girl Fuzzy; I don't know if it's Mitzi or Cinderella. And, my God, wait till you see what she was carrying."

Gerd came into sight, the fourth Fuzzy struggling under one arm and a little kitten, black with a white face, peeping over the crook of his other elbow. He was too stunned with disappointment to look at it with more than vague curiosity.

"They aren't our Fuzzies, Gerd. I never saw any of them before."

"Jack, are you sure."

"Of course I'm sure!" He was indignant. "Don't you think I know my own Fuzzies? Don't you think they'd know me?"

"Where'd the pussy come from?" the corporal wanted to know.

"God knows. They must have picked it up somewhere. She was carrying it in her arms, like a baby."

"They're somebody's Fuzzies. They've been fed Extee Three. We'll take them to the hotel. Whoever it is, I'll bet he misses them as much as I do mine."

His own Fuzzies, whom he would never see again. The full realization didn't hit him until he and Gerd were in the car again. There had been no trace of his Fuzzies from the time they had broken out of their cages at Science Center. This quartet had appeared the night the city police had manufactured the story of the attack on the Lurkin girl, and from the moment they had been seen by the youth who couldn't bring himself to fire on them, they had left a trail that he had been able to pick up at once and follow. Why hadn't his own Fuzzies attracted as much notice in the three weeks since they had vanished?

Because his own Fuzzies didn't exist any more. They had never gotten out of Science Center alive. Somebody Max Fane hadn't been able to question under veridication had murdered them. There was no use, any more, trying to convince himself differently.

"We'll stop at their camp and pick up the blanket and the cushions and the rest of the things. I'll send the people who lost them checks," he said. "The Fuzzies ought to have those things."

XIII

The management of the Hotel Mallory appeared to have undergone a change of heart, or of policy, toward Fuzzies. It might have been Gus Brannhard's threats of action for racial discrimination and the possibility that the Fuzzies might turn out to be a race instead of an animal species after all. The manager might have been shamed by the way the Lurkin story had crumbled into discredit, and influenced by the revived public sympathy for the Fuzzies. Or maybe he just decided that the chartered Zarathustra Company wasn't as omnipotent as he'd believed. At any rate, a large room, usually used for banquets, was made available for the Fuzzies George Lunt and Ben Rainsford were bringing in for the trial, and the four strangers and their black-and-white kitten were installed there. There were a lot of toys of different sorts, courtesy of the management, and a big view screen. The four strange Fuzzies dashed for this immediately and turned it on, yeeking in delight as they watched landing craft coming down and lifting out at the municipal spaceport. They found it very interesting. It only bored the kitten.

With some misgivings, Jack brought Baby down and introduced him. They were delighted with Baby, and Baby thought the kitten was the most wonderful thing he had ever seen. When it was time to feed them, Jack had his own dinner brought in, and ate with them. Gus and Gerd came down and joined him later.

"We got the Lurkin kid and her father," Gus said, and then falsettoed: " 'Naw, Pop gimme a beatin', and the cops told me to say it was the Fuzzies.' "

"She say that?"

"Under verification, with the screen blue as a sapphire, in front of half a dozen witnesses and with audiovisuals on. Interworld's putting it on the air this evening. Her father admitted it, too; named Woller and the desk sergeant. We're still looking for them; till we get them, we aren't any closer to Emmert or Grego. We did pick up the two car cops, but they don't know anything on anybody but Woller."

That was good enough, as far as it went, Brannhard thought, but it didn't go far enough. There were those four strange Fuzzies showing up out of nowhere, right in the middle of Nick Emmert's drive-hunt. They'd been kept somewhere by somebody—that was how they'd learned to eat Extee Three and found out about view-screens. Their appearance was too well synchronized to be accidental. The whole thing smelled to him of a booby trap.

One good thing had happened. Judge Pendarvis had decided that it would be next to impossible, in view of the widespread public interest in the case and the influence of the Zarathustra Company, to get an impartial jury, and had proposed a judicial trial by a panel of three judges, himself one of them. Even Leslie Coombes had felt forced to agree to that.

He told Jack about the decision. Jack listened with apparent attentiveness, and then said:

"You know, Gus, I'll always be glad I let Little Fuzzy smoke my pipe when he wanted to, that night out at camp."

The way he was feeling, he wouldn't have cared less if the case was going to be tried by a panel of three zara-goats.

Ben Rainsford, his two Fuzzies, and George Lunt, Ahmed Khadra and the other constabulary witnesses and their family, arrived shortly before noon on Saturday. The Fuzzies were quartered in the stripped-out banquet room, and quickly made friends with the four already there, and with Baby. Each family bedded down apart, but they ate together and played with each others' toys and sat in a clump to watch the viewscreen. At first, the Ferny Creek family showed jealousy when too much attention was paid to their kitten, until they decided that nobody was trying to steal it.

It would have been a lot of fun, eleven Fuzzies and a Baby Fuzzy and a black-and-white kitten, if Jack hadn't kept seeing his own family, six quiet little ghosts watching but unable to join the frolicking.

Max Fane brightened when he saw who was on his screen.

"Well, Colonel Ferguson, glad to see you."

"Marshal," Ferguson was smiling broadly. "You'll be even gladder in a minute. A couple of my men, from Post Eight, picked up Woller and that desk sergeant, Fuentes."

"Ha!" He started feeling warm inside, as though he had just downed a slug of Baldur honey-rum. "How?"

"Well, you know Nick Emmert has a hunting lodge down there. Post Eight keeps an eye on it for him. This afternoon, one of Lieutenant Obefemi's cars was passing over it, and they picked up some radiation and infrared on their detectors, as though the power was on inside. When they went down to investigate, they found Woller and Fuentes making themselves at home. They brought them in, and both of them admitted under verification that Emmert had given them the keys and sent them down there to hide out till after the trial.

"They denied that Emmert had originated the frame-up. That had been one of Woller's own flashes of genius, but Emmert knew what the score was and went right along with it. They're being brought up here the first thing tomorrow morning."

"Well, that's swell, Colonel! Has it gotten out to the news services yet?"

"No. We would like to have them both questioned here in Mallorysport, and their confessions recorded, before we let the story out. Otherwise, somebody might try to take steps to shut them up for good."

That had been what he had been thinking of. He said so, and Ferguson nodded. Then he hesitated for a moment, and said:

"Max, do you like the situation here in Mallorysport? Be damned if I do."

"What do you mean?"

"There are too many strangers in town," Ian Ferguson said. "All the same kind of strangers—husky-looking young men, twenty to thirty, going around in pairs and small groups. I've been noticing it since day before last, and there seem to be more of them every time I look around."

"Well, Ian, it's a young man's planet, and we can expect a big crowd in town for the trial. . . ."

He didn't really believe that. He just wanted Ian Ferguson to put a name on it first. Ferguson shook his head.

"No, Max. This isn't a trial-day crowd. We both know what they're like; remember when they tried the Gawn brothers? No whooping it up in bars, no excitement, no big crap games; this crowd's just walking around, keeping quiet, as though they expected a word from somebody."

"Infiltration." Goddamit, he'd said it first, himself after all! "Victor Grego's worried about this."

"I know it, Max. And Victor Grego's like a veldbeest bull; he isn't dangerous till he's scared, and then watch out. And against the gang that's moving in here, the men you and I have together would last about as long as a pint of trade-gin at a Sheshan funeral."

"You thinking of pushing the panic-button?"

The constabulary commander frowned. "I don't want to. A dim view would be taken back on Terra if I did it without needing to. Dimmer view would be taken of needing to without doing it, though. I'll make another check, first."

Gerd van Riebeek sorted the papers on the desk into piles, lit a cigarette and then started to mix himself a highball.

"Fuzzies are members of a sapient race," he declared. "They reason logically, both deductively and inductively. They learn by experiment, analysis and association. They formulate general principles, and apply them to specific instances. They plan their activities in advance. They make designed artifacts, and artifacts to make artifacts. They are able to symbolize, and convey ideas in symbolic form, and form symbols by abstracting from objects.

"They have aesthetic sense and creativity," he continued. "They become bored in idleness, and they enjoy solving problems for the pleasure of solving them. They bury their dead ceremoniously, and bury artifacts with them."

He blew a smoke ring, and then tasted his drink. "They

do all these things, and they also do carpenter work, blow police whistles, make eating tools to eat land-prawns with and put molecule-model balls together. Obviously they are sapient beings. But don't, *please* don't ask me to define sapience, because God damn it to Nifflheim, I still can't!"

"I think you just did," Jack said.

"No, that won't do. I need a definition."

"Don't worry, Gerd," Gus Brannhard told him. "Leslie Combes will bring a nice shiny new definition into court. We'll just use that."

XIV

They walked together, Frederic and Claudette Pendarvis, down through the roof garden toward the landing stage, and, as she always did, Claudette stopped and cut a flower and fastened it in his lapel.

"Will the Fuzzies be in court?" she asked.

"Oh, they'll have to be. I don't know about this morning; it'll be mostly formalities." He made a grimace that was half a frown and half a smile. "I really don't know whether to consider them as witnesses or as exhibits, and I hope I'm not called on to rule on that, at least at the start. Either way, Coombes or Brannhard would accuse me of showing prejudice."

"I want to see them. I've seen them on screen, but I want to see them for real."

"You haven't been in one of my courts for a long time, Claudette. If I find that they'll be brought in today, I'll call you. I'll even abuse my position to the extent of arranging for you to see them outside the courtroom. Would you like that?"

She'd love it. Claudette had a limitless capacity for delight in things like that. They kissed good-bye, and he went to where his driver was holding open the door of the aircar and got in. At a thousand feet he looked back; she was still standing at the edge of the roof garden, looking up.

He'd have to find out whether it would be safe for her to come in. Max Fane was worried about the possibility of trouble, and so was Ian Ferguson, and neither was given to timorous imaginings. As the car began to descend toward the Central Courts buildings, he saw that there were guards on the roof, and they weren't just carrying pistols — he caught the glint of rifle barrels, and the twinkle of steel helmets. Then, as he came in, he saw that their uniforms were a lighter shade of blue than the constabulary wore. Ankle boots and red-striped trousers; Space Marines in

143

dress blues. So Ian Ferguson had pushed the button. It occurred to him that Claudette might be safer here than at home.

A sergeant and a couple of men came up as he got out; the sergeant touched the beak of his helmet in the nearest thing to a salute a Marine ever gave anybody in civilian clothes.

"Judge Pendarvis? Good morning, sir."

"Good morning, sergeant. Just why are Federation Marines guarding the court building?"

"Standing by, sir. Orders of Commodore Napier. You'll find that Marshal Fane's people are in charge below-decks, but Marine Captain Casagra and Navy Captain Greibenfeld are waiting to see you in your office."

As he started toward the elevators, a big Zarathustra Company car was coming in. The sergeant turned quickly, beckoned a couple of his men and went toward it on the double. He wondered what Leslie Coombes would think about those Marines.

The two officers in his private chambers were both wearing sidearms. So, also, was Marshal Fane, who was with them. They all rose to greet him, sitting down when he was at his desk. He asked the same question he had of the sergeant above.

"Well, Constabulary Colonel Ferguson called Commodore Napier last evening and requested armed assistance, your Honor," the officer in Space Navy black said. "He suspected, he said, that the city had been infiltrated. In that, your Honor, he was perfectly correct; beginning Wednesday afternoon, Marine Captain Casagra, here, on Commodore Napier's orders, began landing a Marine infiltration force, preparatory to taking over the Residency. That's been accomplished now; Commodore Napier is there, and both Resident General Emmert and Attorney General O'Brien are under arrest, on a variety of malfeasance and corrupt-practice charges, but that won't come into your Honor's court. They'll be sent back to Terra for trial."

"Then Commodore Napier's taken over the civil government?"

"Well, say he's assumed control of it, pending the outcome of this trial. We want to know whether the present administration's legal or not."

"Then you won't interfere with the trial itself?"

"That depends, your Honor. We are certainly going to participate." He looked at his watch. "You won't convene court for another hour? Then perhaps I'll have time to explain."

Max Fane met them at the courtroom door with a pleasant greeting. Then he saw Baby Fuzzy on Jack's shoulder and looked dubious.

"I don't know about him, Jack. I don't think he'll be allowed in the courtroom."

"Nonsense!" Gus Brannhard told him. "I admit, he is both a minor child and an incompetent aborigine, but he is the only surviving member of the family of the decedent Jane Doe alias Goldilocks, and as such has an indisputable right to be present."

"Well, just as long as you keep him from sitting on people's heads. Gus, you and Jack sit over there; Ben, you and Gerd find seats in the witness section."

It would be half an hour till court would convene, but already the spectators' seats were full, and so was the balcony. The jury box, on the left of the bench, was occupied by a number of officers in Navy black and Marine blue. Since there would be no jury, they had apparently appropriated it for themselves. The press box was jammed and bristling with equipment.

Baby was looking up interestedly at the big screen behind the judges' seats; while transmitting the court scene to the public, it also showed, like a nonreversing mirror, the same view to the spectators. Baby wasn't long in identifying himself in it, and waved his arms excitedly. At that moment, there was a bustle at the door by which they had entered, and Leslie Coombes came in, followed by Ernst Mallin and a couple of his assistants, Ruth Ortheris, Juan Jimenez —and Leonard Kellogg. The last time he had seen Kellogg had been at George Lunt's complaint court, his face bandaged and his feet in a pair of borrowed moccasins because his shoes, stained with the blood of Goldilocks, had been impounded as evidence.

Coombes glanced toward the table where he and Brannhard were sitting, caught sight of Baby waving to himself in the big screen and turned to Fane with an indignant protest. Fane shook his head. Coombes protested again, and drew another headshake. Finally he shrugged and led Kellogg to the table reserved for them, where they sat down.

Once Pendarvis and his two associates—a short, round-faced man on his right, a tall, slender man with white hair and a black mustache on his left—were seated, the trial got underway briskly. The charges were read, and then Brannhard, as the Kellogg prosecutor, addressed the court —"being known as Goldilocks . . . sapient member of a sapient race . . . willful and deliberate act of the said Leonard Kellogg . . . brutal and unprovoked murder." He backed away, sat on the edge of the table and picked up Baby Fuzzy, fondling him while Leslie Coombes accused Jack Holloway· of brutally assaulting the said Leonard Kellogg and ruthlessly shooting down Kurt Borch.

"Well, gentlemen, I believe we can now begin hearing the witnesses," the Chief Justice said. "Who will start prosecuting whom?"

Gus handed Baby to Jack and went forward; Coombes stepped up beside him.

"Your Honor, this entire trial hinges upon the question of whether a member of the species *Fuzzy fuzzy holloway zarathustra* is or is not a sapient being," Gus said. "However, before any attempt is made to determine this question, we should first establish, by testimony, just what happened at Holloway's Camp, in Cold Creek Valley, on the afternoon of June 19, Atomic Era Six Fifty-Four, and once this is established, we can then proceed to the question of whether or not the said Goldilocks was truly a sapient being."

"I agree," Coombes said equably. "Most of these witnesses will have to be recalled to the stand later, but in general I think Mr. Brannhard's suggestion will be economical of the court's time."

"Will Mr. Coombes agree to stipulate that any evidence tending to prove or disprove the sapience of Fuzzies in general be accepted as proving or disproving the sapience of the being referred to as Goldilocks?"

Coombes looked that over carefully, decided that it wasn't booby-trapped and agreed. A deputy marshal went over to the witness stand, made some adjustments and snapped on a switch at the back of the chair. Immediately the two-foot globe in a standard behind it lit, a clear blue. George Lunt's name was called; the lieutenant took his seat and the bright helmet was let down over his head and the electrodes attached.

The globe stayed a calm, untroubled blue while he stated his name and rank. Then he waited while Coombes and Brannhard conferred. Finally Brannhard took a silver half-sol piece from his pocket, shook it between cupped palms and slapped it onto his wrist. Coombes said, "Heads," and Brannhard uncovered it, bowed slightly and stepped back.

"Now, Lieutenant Lunt," Coombes began, "when you arrived at the temporary camp across the run from Holloway's camp, what did you find there?"

"Two dead people," Lunt said. "A Terran human, who had been shot three times through the chest, and a Fuzzy, who had been kicked or trampled to death."

"Your Honors!" Coombes expostulated, "I must ask that the witness be requested to rephrase his answer, and that the answer he has just made be stricken from the record. The witness, under the circumstances, has no right to refer to the Fuzzies as 'people.'"

"Your Honors," Brannhard caught it up, "Mr. Coombes's objection is no less prejudicial. He has no right, under the circumstances, to deny that the Fuzzies be referred to as 'people.' This is tantamount to insisting that the witness speak of them as nonsapient animals."

It went on like that for five minutes. Jack began doodling on a notepad. Baby picked up a pencil with both hands and began making doodles too. They looked rather like the knots he had been learning to tie. Finally, the court intervened and told Lunt to tell, in his own words, why he went to Holloway's camp, what he found there, what he was told and what he did. There was some argument between Coombes and Brannhard, at one point, about the difference between hearsay and *res gestae*. When he was through, Coombes said, "No questions."

"Lieutenant, you placed Leonard Kellogg under arrest on a complaint of homicide by Jack Holloway. I take it that you considered this complaint a valid one?"

147

"Yes, sir. I believed that Leonard Kellogg had killed a sapient being. Only sapient beings bury their dead."

Ahmed Khadra testified. The two troopers who had come in the other car, and the men who had brought the investigative equipment and done the photographing at the scene testified. Brannhard called Ruth Ortheris to the stand, and, after some futile objections by Coombes, she was allowed to tell her own story of the killing of Goldilocks, the beating of Kellogg and the shooting of Borch. When she had finished, the Chief Justice rapped with his gavel.

"I believe that this testimony is sufficient to establish the fact tht the being referred to as Jane Doe alias Goldilocks was in fact kicked and trampled to death by the defendant Leonard Kellogg, and that the Terran human known as Kurt Borch was in fact shot to death by Jack Holloway. This being the case, we may now consider whether or not either or both of these killings constitute murder within the meaning of the law. It is now eleven forty. We will adjourn for lunch, and court will reconvene at fourteen hundred. There are a number of things, including some alterations to the courtroom, which must be done before the afternoon session . . . Yes, Mr. Brannhard?"

"Your Honors, there is only one member of the species *Fuzzy fuzzy holloway zarathustra* at present in court, an immature and hence nonrepresentative individual." He picked up Baby and exhibited him. "If we are to take up the question of the sapience of this species, or race, would it not be well to send for the Fuzzies now staying at the Hotel Mallory and have them on hand?"

"Well, Mr. Brannhard," Pendarvis said, "we will certainly want Fuzzies in court, but let me suggest that we wait until after court reconvenes before sending for them. It may be that they will not be needed this afternoon. Anything else?" He tapped with his gavel. "Then court is adjourned until fourteen hundred."

Some alterations in the courtroom had been a conservative way of putting it. Four rows of spectators' seats had been abolished, and the dividing rail moved back. The witness chair, originally at the side of the bench, had been moved to the dividing rail and now faced the bench, and a large number of tables had been brought in and ranged in an arc with the witness chair in the middle of it. Everybody at the tables could face the judges, and also see everybody else by looking into the big screen. A witness on the chair could also see the veridicator in the same way.

Gus Brannhard looked around, when he entered with Jack, and swore softly.

"No wonder they gave us two hours for lunch. I wonder what the idea is." Then he gave a short laugh. "Look at Coombes; he doesn't like it a bit."

A deputy with a seating diagram came up to them.

"Mr. Brannard, you and Mr. Holloway over here, at this table." He pointed to one a little apart from the others, at the extreme right facing the bench. "And Dr. van Riebeek, and Dr. Rainsford over here, please."

The court crier's loud-speaker, overhead, gave two sharp whistles and began:

"Now hear this! Now hear this! Court will convene in five minutes—"

Brannhard's head jerked around instantly, and Jack's eyes followed his. The court crier was a Space Navy petty officer.

"What the devil is this?" Brannhard demanded. "A Navy court-martial?"

"That's what I've been wondering, Mr. Brannhard," the deputy said. "They've taken over the whole planet, you know."

"Maybe we're in luck, Gus. I've always heard that if you're innocent you're better off before a court-martial and if you're guilty you're better off in a civil court."

He saw Leslie Coombes and Leonard Kellogg being seated at a similar table at the opposite side of the bench. Apparently Coombes had also heard that. The seating arrangements at the other tables seemed a little odd too. Gerd van Reibeek was next to Ruth Ortheris, and Ernst Mallin was next to Ben Rainsford, with Juan Jimenez on his other side. Gus was looking up at the balcony.

"I'll bet every lawyer on the planet's taking this in," he said. "Oh-oh! See the white-haired lady in the blue dress, Jack? That's the Chief Justice's wife. This is the first time she's been in court for years."

"Hear ye! Hear ye! Hear ye! Rise for the Honorable Court!"

Somebody must have given the petty officer a quick briefing on courtroom phraseology. He stood up, holding Baby Fuzzy, while the three judges filed in and took their seats. As soon as they sat down, the Chief Justice rapped briskly with his gavel.

"In order to forestall a spate of objections, I want to say that these present arrangements are temporary, and so will be the procedures which will be followed. We are not, at the moment, trying Jack Holloway or Leonard Kellogg. For the rest of this day, and, I fear, for a good many days to come, we will be concerned exclusively with determining the level of mentation of *Fuzzy fuzzy holloway zarathustra.*

"For this purpose, we are temporarily abandoning some of the traditional trial procedures. We will call witnesses; statements of purported fact will be made under veridication as usual. We will also have a general discussion, in which all of you at these tables will be free to participate. I and my associates will preside; as we can't have everybody shouting disputations at once, anyone wishing to speak will have to be recognized. At least, I hope we will be able to conduct the discussion in this manner.

"You will all have noticed the presence of a number of officers from Xerxes Naval Base, and I suppose you have all heard that Commodore Napier has assumed control of the civil government. Captain Greibenfeld, will you please rise and be seen? He is here participating as *amicus curiae,* and I have given him the right to question witnesses and to delegate that right to any of his officers he may deem proper. Mr. Coombes and Mr. Brannhard may also delegate that right as they see fit."

Coombes was on his feet at once. "Your Honors, if we are now to discuss the sapience question, I would suggest that the first item on our order of business be the presentation of some acceptable definition of sapience. I should, for my part, very much like to know what it is that the Kellogg prosecution and the Holloway defense mean when they use that term."

That's it. They want us to define it. Gerd van Riebeek

was looking chagrined; Ernst Mallin was smirking. Gus Brannhard, however, was pleased.

"Jack, they haven't any more damn definition than we do," he whispered.

Captain Greibenfeld, who had seated himself after rising at the request of the court, was on his feet again.

"Your Honors, during the past month we at Xerxes Naval Base have been working on exactly that problem. We have a very considerable interest in having the classification of this planet established, and we also feel that this may not be the last time a question of disputable sapience may arise. I believe, your Honors, that we have approached such a definition. However, before we begin discussing it, I would like the court's permission to present a demonstration which may be of help in understanding the problems involved."

"Captain Greibenfeld has already discussed this demonstration with me, and it has my approval. Will you please proceed, Captain," the Chief Justice said.

Greibenfeld nodded, and a deputy marshal opened the door on the right of the bench. Two spacemen came in, carrying cartons. One went up to the bench; the other started around in front of the tables, distributing small battery-powered hearing aids.

"Please put them in your ears and turn them on," he said. "Thank you."

Baby Fuzzy tried to get Jack's. He put the plug in his ear and switched on the power. Instantly he began hearing a number of small sounds he had never heard before, and Baby was saying to him: *"He-inta sa-wa'aka; igga sa geeda?"*

"Muhgawd, Gus, he's talking!"

"Yes, I hear him; what do you suppose —?"

"Ultrasonic; God, why didn't we think of that long ago?"

He snapped off the hearing aid. Baby Fuzzy was saying, "Yeeck." When he turned it on again, Baby was saying, *"Kukk-ina za zeeva."*

"No, Baby, Pappy Jack doesn't understand. We'll have to be awfully patient, and learn each other's language."

"Pa-pee Jaaak!" Baby cried. *"Ba-bee za-hinga; Pa-pee Jaak za zag ga he-izza!"*

151

"That yeeking is just the audible edge of their speech; bet we have a lot of transsonic tones in our voices, too."

"Well, he can hear what we say; he's picked up his name and yours."

"Mr. Brannhard, Mr. Holloway," Judge Pendarvis was saying, "may we please have your attention? Now, have you all your earplugs in and turned on? Very well; carry on, Captain."

This time, an ensign went out and came back with a crowd of enlisted men, who had six Fuzzies with them. They set them down in the open space between the bench and the arc of tables and backed away. The Fuzzies drew together into a clump and stared around them, and he stared, unbelievingly, at them. They couldn't be; they didn't exist any more. But they were —Little Fuzzy and Mamma Fuzzy and Mike and Mitzi and Ko-Ko and Cinderella. Baby whooped something and leaped from the table, and Mamma came stumbling to meet him, clasping him in her arms. Then they all saw him and began clamoring: *"Pa-pee Jaaak! Pa-pee Jaaak!"*

He wasn't aware of rising and leaving the table; the next thing he realized, he was sitting on the floor, his family mobbing him and hugging him, gabbling with joy. Dimly he heard the gavel hammering, and the voice of Chief Justice Pendarvis: "Court is recessed for ten minutes!" By that time, Gus was with him; gathering the family up, they carried them over to their table.

They stumbled and staggered when they moved, and that frightened him for a moment. Then he realized that they weren't sick or drugged. They'd just been in low-G for a while and hadn't become reaccustomed to normal weight. Now he knew why he hadn't been able to find any trace of them. He noticed that each of them was wearing a little shoulder bag—a Marine Corps first-aid pouch—slung from a webbing strap. Why the devil hadn't he thought of making them something like that? He touched one and commented, trying to pitch his voice as nearly like theirs as he could. They all babbled in reply and began opening the little bags and showing him what they had in them—little knives and miniature tools and bits of bright or colored junk they had picked up. Little Fuzzy produced a tiny pipe with a hardwood bowl, and a little pouch of

152

tobacco from which he filled it. Finally, he got out a small lighter.

"Your Honors!" Gus shouted, "I know court is recessed, but please observe what Little Fuzzy is doing."

While they watched, Little Fuzzy snapped the lighter and held the flame to the pipe bowl, puffing.

Across on the other side, Leslie Coombes swallowed once or twice and closed his eyes.

When Pendarvis rapped for attention and declared court reconvened, he said:

"Ladies and gentlemen, you have all seen and heard this demonstration of Captain Greibenfeld's. You have heard these Fuzzies uttering what certainly sounds like meaningful speech, and you have seen one of them light a pipe and smoke. Incidentally, while smoking in court is discountenanced, we are going to make an exception, during this trial, in favor of Fuzzies. Other people will please not feel themselves discriminated against."

That brought Coombes to his feet with a rush. He started around the table and then remembered that under the new rules he didn't have to.

"Your Honors, I objected strongly to the use of that term by a witness this morning; I must object even more emphatically to its employment from the bench. I have indeed heard these Fuzzies make sounds which might be mistaken for words, but I must deny that this is true speech. As to this trick of using a lighter, I will undertake, in not more than thirty days, to teach it to any Terran primate or Freyan kholph."

Greibenfeld rose immediately. "Your Honors, in the past thirty days, while these Fuzzies were at Xerxes Naval Base, we have compiled a vocabulary of a hundred-odd Fuzzy words, for all of which definite meanings have been established, and a great many more for which we have not as yet learned the meanings. We even have the beginning of a Fuzzy grammar. As for this so-called trick of using a lighter, Little Fuzzy—we didn't know his name then and referred to him as M2—learned that for himself, by observation. We didn't teach him to smoke a pipe either; he knew that before we had anything to do with him."

Jack rose while Greibenfeld was still speaking. As soon as the Space Navy captain had finished, he said:

"Captain Greibenfeld, I want to thank you and your people for taking care of the Fuzzies, and I'm very glad you learned how to hear what they're saying, and thank you for all the nice things you gave them, but why couldn't you have let me know they were safe? I haven't been very happy the last month, you know."

"I know that, Mr. Holloway, and if it's any comfort to you, we were all very sorry for you, but we could not take the risk of compromising our secret intelligence agent in the Company's Science Center, the one who smuggled the Fuzzies out the morning after their escape." He looked quickly across in front of the bench to the table at the other end of the arc. Kellogg was sitting with his face in his hands, oblivious to everything that was going on, but Leslie Coombes's well-disciplined face had broken, briefly, into a look of consternation. "By the time you and Mr. Brannhard and Marshal Fane arrived with an order of the court for the Fuzzies' recovery, they had already been taken from Science Center and were on a Navy landing craft for Xerxes. We couldn't do anything without exposing our agent. That, I am glad to say, is no longer a consideration."

"Well, Captain Greibenfeld," the Chief Justice said, "I assume you mean to introduce further testimony about the observations and studies made by your people on Xerxes. For the record, we'd like to have it established that they were actually taken there, and when, and how."

"Yes, your Honor. If you will call the fourth name on the list I gave you, and allow me to do the questioning, we can establish that."

The Chief Justice picked up a paper. "Lieutenant j.g. Ruth Ortheris, TFN Reserve," he called out.

This time, Jack Holloway looked up into the big screen, in which he could see everybody. Gerd van Riebeek, who had been trying to ignore the existence of the woman beside him, had turned to stare at her in amazement. Coombes's face was ghastly for an instant, then froze into corpselike immobility: Ernst Mallin was dithering in incredulous anger; beside him Ben Rainsford was grinning in just as incredulous delight. As Ruth came around in front of the bench, the Fuzzies gave her an ovation; they re-

154

membered and liked her. Gus Brannhard was gripping his arm and saying: "Oh, brother! This is it, Jack; it's all over but shooting the cripples!"

Lieutenant j.g. Ortheris, under a calmly blue globe, testified to coming to Zarathustra as a Federation Naval Reserve officer recalled to duty with Intelligence, and taking a position with the Company.

"As a regularly qualified doctor of psychology, I worked under Dr. Mallin in the scientific division, and also with the school department and the juvenile court. At the same time I was regularly transmitting reports to Commander Aelborg, the chief of Intelligence on Xerxes. The object of this surveillance was to make sure that the Zarathustra Company was not violating the provisions of their charter or Federation law. Until the middle of last month, I had nothing to report beyond some rather irregular financial transactions involving Resident General Emmert. Then, on the evening of June fifteen—"

That was when Ben had transmitted the tape to Juan Jimenez; she described how it had come to her attention.

"As soon as possible, I transmitted a copy of this tape to Commander Aelborg. The next night, I called Xerxes from the screen on Dr. van Riebeek's boat and reported what I'd learned about the Fuzzies. I was then informed that Leonard Kellogg had gotten hold of a copy of the Holloway-Rainsford tape and had alerted Victor Grego; that Kellogg and Ernst Mallin were being sent to Beta Continent with instructions to prevent publication of any report claiming sapience for the Fuzzies and to fabricate evidence to support an accusation that Dr. Rainsford and Mr. Holloway were perpetrating a deliberate scientific hoax."

"Here, I'll have to object to this, your Honor," Coombes said, rising. "This is nothing but hearsay."

"This is part of a Navy Intelligence situation estimate given to Lieutenant Ortheris, based on reports we had received from other agents." Captain Greibenfeld said. "She isn't the only one we have on Zarathustra, you know. Mr. Coombes, if I hear another word of objection to this officer's testimony from you, I am going to ask Mr. Brannhard to subpoena Victor Grego and question him under veridication about it."

"Mr. Brannhard will be more than happy to oblige, Commander," Gus said loudly and distinctly.

Coombes sat down hastily.

"Well, Lieutenant Ortheris, this is most interesting, but at the moment, what we're trying to establish is how these Fuzzies got to Xerxes Naval Base," the chubby associate justice, Ruiz, put in.

"I'll try to get them there as quickly as possible, your Honor," she said. "On the night of Friday the twenty-second, the Fuzzies were taken from Mr. Holloway and brought into Mallorysport; they were turned over by Mohammed O'Brien to Juan Jimenez, who took them to Science Center and put them in cages in a room back of his office. They immediately escaped. I found them, the next morning, and was able to get them out of the building, and to turn them over to Commander Aelborg, who had come down from Xerxes to take personal charge of the Fuzzy operation. I will not testify as to how I was able to do this. I am at present and was then an officer of the Terran Federation Armed Forces; the courts have no power to compel a Federation officer to give testimony involving breach of military security. I was informed, through my contact in Mallorysport, from time to time, of the progress of the work of measuring the Fuzzies' mental level there; I was able to pass on suggestions occasionally. Any time any of these suggestions was based on ideas originating with Dr. Mallin, I was careful to give him full credit.'"

Mallin looked singularly unappreciative.

Brannhard got up. "Before this witness is excused, I'd like to ask if she knows anything about four other Fuzzies, the ones found by Jack Holloway up Ferny Creek on Friday."

"Why, yes; they're my Fuzzies, and I was worried about them. Their names are Complex, Syndrome, Id and Superego."

"Your Fuzzies, Lieutenant?"

"Well, I took care of them and worked with them; Juan Jimenez and some Company hunters caught them over on Beta Continent. They were kept at a farm center about five hundred miles north of here, which had been vacated for the purpose. I spent all my time with them, and Dr.

156

Mallin was with them most of the time. Then, on Monday night, Mr. Coombes came and got them."

"Mr. Coombes, did you say?" Gus Brannhard asked.

"Mr. Leslie Coombes, the Company attorney. He said they were needed in Mallorysport. It wasn't till the next day that I found out what they were needed for. They'd been turned loose in front of that Fuzzy hunt, in the hope that they would be killed."

She looked across at Coombes; if looks were bullets, he'd have been deader than Kurt Borch.

"Why would they sacrifice four Fuzzies merely to support a story that was bound to come apart anyhow?" Brannhard asked.

"That was no sacrifice. They had to get rid of those Fuzzies, and they were afraid to kill them themselves for fear they'd be charged with murder along with Leonard Kellogg. Everybody, from Ernst Mallin down, who had anything to do with them was convinced of their sapience. For one thing, we'd been using those hearing aids ourselves; I suggested it, after getting the idea from Xerxes. Ask Dr. Mallin about it, under veridication. Ask him about the multiordinal polyencephalograph experiments, too."

"Well, we have the Holloway Fuzzies placed on Xerxes," the Chief Justice said. "We can hear the testimony of the people who worked with them there at any time. Now, I want to hear from Dr. Ernest Mallin."

Coombes was on his feet again. "Your Honors, before any further testimony is heard, I would like to confer with my client privately."

"I fail to see any reason why we should interrupt proceedings for that purpose, Mr. Coombes. You can confer as much as you wish with your client after this session, and I can assure you that you will be called upon to do nothing on his behalf until then." He gave a light tap with his gavel and then said: "Dr. Ernst Mallin will please take the stand."

XV

Ernst Mallin shrank, as though trying to pull himself into himself, when he heard his name. He didn't want to testify. He had been dreading this moment for days. Now he would have to sit in that chair, and they would ask him questions, and he couldn't answer them truthfully and the globe over his head—

When the deputy marshal touched his shoulder and spoke to him, he didn't think, at first, that his legs would support him. It seemed miles, with all the staring faces on either side of him. Somehow, he reached the chair and sat down, and they fitted the helmet over his head and attached the electrodes. They used to make a witness take some kind of an oath to tell the truth. They didn't any more. They didn't need to.

As soon as the veridicator was on, he looked up at the big screen behind the four judges; the globe above his head was a glaring red. There was a titter of laughter. Nobody in the courtroom knew better than he what was happening. He had screens in his laboratory that broke it all down into individual patterns—the steady pulsing waves from the cortex, the alpha and beta waves; beta-aleph and beta-beth and beta-gimel and beta-daleth. The thalamic waves. He thought of all of them, and of the electromagnetic events which accompanied brain activity. As he did, the red faded and the globe became blue. He was no longer suppressing statements and substituting other statements he knew to be false. If he could keep it that way. But, sooner or later, he knew, he wouldn't be able to.

The globe stayed blue while he named himself and stated his professional background. There was a brief flicker of red while he was listing his publication—that paper, entirely the work of one of his students, which he had published under his own name. He had forgotten about that, but his conscience hadn't.

"Dr. Mallin," the oldest of the three judges, who sat in

the middle, began, "what, in your professional opinion, is the difference between sapient and nonsapient mentation?"

"The ability to think consciously," he stated. The globe stayed blue.

"Do you mean that nonsapient animals aren't conscious, or do you mean they don't think?"

"Well, neither. Any life form with a central nervous system has some consciousness—awareness of existence and of its surroundings. And anything having a brain thinks, to use the term at its loosest. What I meant was that only the sapient mind thinks and knows that it is thinking."

He was perfectly safe so far. He talked about sensory stimuli and responses, and about conditioned reflexes. He went back to the first century Pre-Atomic, and Pavlov and Korzybski and Freud. The globe never flickered.

"The nonsapient animal is conscious only of what is immediately present to the senses and responds automatically. It will perceive something and make a single statement about it—this is good to eat, this sensation is unpleasant, this is a sex-gratification object, this is dangerous. The sapient mind, on the other hand, is conscious of thinking about these sense stimuli, and makes descriptive statements about them, and then makes statements about those statements, in a connected chain. I have a structural differential at my seat; if somebody will bring it to me—"

"Well, never mind now, Dr. Mallin. When you're off the stand and the discussion begins you can show what you mean. We just want your opinion in general terms, now."

"Well, the sapient mind can generalize. To the nonsapient animal, every experience is either totally novel or identical with some remembered experience. A rabbit will flee from one dog because to the rabbit mind it is identical with another dog that has chased it. A bird will be attracted to an apple, and each apple will be a unique red thing to peck at. The sapient being will say, 'These red objects are apples; as a class, they are edible and flavorsome.' He sets up a class under the general label of apples. This, in turn, leads to the formation of abstract ideas—redness, flavor, et cetera—conceived of apart from any specific physical object, and to the ordering of abstractions—'fruit' as

159

distinguished from apples, 'food' as distinguished from fruit."

The globe was still placidly blue. The three judges waited, and he continued:

"Having formed these abstract ideas, it becomes necessary to symbolize them, in order to deal with them apart from the actual object. The sapient being is a symbolizer, and a symbol communicator; he is able to convey to other sapient beings his ideas in symbolic form."

"Like *Pa-pee Jaak*?" the judge on his right, with the black mustache, asked.

The globe flashed red at once.

"Your Honors, I cannot consider words picked up at random and learned by rote speech. The Fuzzies have merely learned to associate that sound with a specific human, and use it as a signal, not a as a symbol."

The globe was still red. The Chief Justice, in the middle, rapped with his gavel.

"Dr. Mallin! Of all the people on this planet, you at least should know the impossibility of lying under veridication. Other people just know it can't be done; you know why. Now I'm going to rephrase Judge Janiver's question, and I'll expect you to answer truthfully. If you don't I'm going to hold you in contempt. When those Fuzzies cried out, 'Pappy Jack!' do you or do you not believe that they were using a verbal expression which stood, in their minds, for Mr. Holloway?"

He couldn't say it. This sapience was all a big fake; he had to believe that. The Fuzzies were only little mindless animals.

But he didn't believe it. He knew better. He gulped for a moment.

"Yes, your Honor. The term 'Pappy Jack' is, in their minds, a symbol standing for Mr. Jack Holloway."

He looked at the globe. The red had turned to mauve, the mauve was becoming violet, and then clear blue. He felt better than he had felt since the afternoon Leonard Kellogg had told him about the Fuzzies.

"Then Fuzzies do think consciously, Dr. Mallin?" That was Pendarvis.

"Oh, yes. The fact that they use verbal symbols indicates that, even without other evidence. And the instru-

160

mental evidence was most impressive. The mentation pictures we got by encephalography compare very favorably with those of any human child of ten or twelve years old, and so does their learning and puzzle-solving ability. On puzzles, they always think the problem out first, and then do the mechanical work with about the same mental effort, say, as a man washing his hands or tying his neck-cloth."

The globe was perfectly blue. Mallin had given up trying to lie; he was simply gushing out everything he thought.

Leonard Kellogg slumped forward, his head buried in his elbows on the table, and misery washed over him in tides.

I am a murderer; I killed a person. Only a funny little person with fur, but she was a person, and I knew it when I killed her, I knew it when I saw that little grave out in the woods, and they'll put me in that chair and make me admit it to everybody, and then they'll take me out in the jail yard and somebody will shoot me through the head with a pistol, and—

And all the poor little thing wanted was to show me her new jingle!

"Does anybody want to ask the witness any questions?" the Chief Justice was asking.

"I don't," Captain Greibenfeld said. "Do you, Lieutenant?"

"No, I don't think so," Lieutenant Ybarra said. "Dr. Mallin's given us a very lucid statement of his opinions."

He had, at that, after he'd decided he couldn't beat the veridicator. Jack found himself sympathizing with Mallin. He'd disliked the man from the first, but he looked different now—sort of cleaned and washed out inside. Maybe everybody ought to be veridicated, now and then, to teach them that honesty begins with honesty to self.

"Mr. Coombes?" Mr. Coombes looked as though he never wanted to ask another witness another question as long as he lived. "Mr. Brannhard?"

Gus got up, holding a sapient member of a sapient race who was hanging onto his beard, and thanked Ernst Mallin fulsomely.

"In that case, we'll adjourn until o-nine-hundred tomorrow. Mr. Coombes, I have here a check on the chartered Zarathustra Company for twenty-five thousand sols. I am returning it to you and I am canceling Dr. Kellogg's bail," Judge Pendarvis said, as a couple of attendants began getting Mallin loose from the veridicator.

"Are you also canceling Jack Holloway's?"

"No, and I would advise you not to make an issue of it, Mr. Coombes. The only reason I haven't dismissed the charge against Mr. Holloway is that I don't want to handicap you by cutting off your foothold in the prosecution. I do not consider Mr. Holloway a bail risk. I do so consider your client, Dr. Kellogg."

"Frankly, your Honor, so do I," Coombes admitted. "My protest was merely an example of what Dr. Mallin would call conditioned reflex."

Then a crowd began pushing up around the table; Ben Rainsford, George Lunt and his troopers, Gerd and Ruth, shoving in among them, their arms around each other.

"We'll be at the hotel after a while, Jack," Gerd was saying. "Ruth and I are going out for a drink and something to eat; we'll be around later to pick up her Fuzzies."

Now his partner had his girl back, and his partner's girl had a Fuzzy family of her own. This was going to be real fun. What were their names now? Syndrome, Complex, Id and Superego. The things some people named Fuzzies!

XVI

They stopped whispering at the door, turned right, and ascended to the bench, bearing themselves like images in a procession, Ruiz first, then himself and then Janiver. They turned to the screen so that the public whom they served might see the faces of the judges, and then sat down. The court crier began his chant. They could almost feel the tension in the courtroom. Yves Janiver whispered to them:

"They all know about it."

As soon as the crier had stopped, Max Fane approached the bench, his face blankly expressionless.

"Your Honors, I am ashamed to have to report that the defendant, Leonard Kellogg, cannot be produced in court. He is dead; he committed suicide in his cell last night. While in my custody," he added bitterly.

The stir that went through the courtroom was not shocked surprise, it was a sigh of fulfilled expectation. They all knew about it.

"How did this happen, Marshal?" he asked, almost conversationally.

"The prisoner was put in a cell by himself; there was a pickup eye, and one of my deputies was keeping him under observation by screen." Fane spoke in a toneless, almost robotlike voice. "At twenty-two thirty, the prisoner went to bed, still wearing his shirt. He pulled the blankets up over his head. The deputy observing him thought nothing of that; many prisoners do that, on account of the light. He tossed about for a while, and then appeared to fall asleep.

"When a guard went in to rouse him this morning, the cot, under the blanket, was found saturated with blood. Kellogg had cut his throat, by sawing the zipper track of his shirt back and forth till he severed his jugular vein. He was dead."

"Good heavens, Marshal!" He was shocked. The way

163

he'd heard it, Kellogg had hidden a penknife, and he was prepared to be severe with Fane about it. But a thing like this! He found himself fingering the toothed track of his own jacket zipper. "I don't believe you can be at all censured for not anticipating a thing like that. It isn't a thing anybody would expect."

Janiver and Ruiz spoke briefly in agreement. Marshal Fane bowed slightly and went off to one side.

Leslie Coombes, who seemed to be making a very considerable effort to look grieved and shocked, rose.

"Your Honors, I find myself here without a client." he said. "In fact, I find myself here without any business at all; the case against Mr. Holloway is absolutely insupportable. He shot a man who was trying to kill him, and that's all there is to it. I therefore pray your Honors to dismiss the case against him and discharge him from custody."

Captain Greibenfeld bounded to his feet.

"Your Honors, I fully realized that the defendant is now beyond the jurisdiction of this court, but let me point out that I and my associates are here participating in this case in the hope that the classification of this planet may be determined, and some adequate definition of sapience established. These are most serious questions, your Honors."

"But, your Honors," Coombes protested, "we can't go through the farce of trying a dead man."

"*People of the Colony of Baphomet* versus *Jamshar Singh, Deceased,* charge of arson and sabotage, A.E. 604," the Honorable Gustavus Adolphus Brannhard interrupted.

Yes, you could find a precedent in colonial law for almost anything.

Jack Holloway was on his feet, a Fuzzy cradled in the crook of his left arm, his white mustache bristling truculently.

"I am not a dead man, your Honors, and I am on trial here. The reason I'm not dead is why I am on trial. My defense is that I shot Kurt Borch while he was aiding and abetting in the killing of a Fuzzy. I want it established in this court that it is murder to kill a Fuzzy."

The judge nodded slowly. "I will not dismiss the charges against Mr. Holloway," he said. "Mr. Holloway had been arraigned on a charge of murder; if he is not guilty, he is entitled to the vindication of an acquittal. I am afraid, Mr. Coombes, that you will have to go on prosecuting him."

Another brief stir, like a breath of wind over a grain field, ran through the courtroom. The show was going on after all.

All the Fuzzies were in court this morning; Jack's six, and the five from the constabulary post, and Ben's Flora and Fauna, and the four Ruth Ortheris claimed. There was too much discussion going on for anybody to keep an eye on them. Finally one of the constabulary Fuzzies, either Dillinger or Dr. Crippen, and Ben Rainsford's Flora and Fauna, came sauntering out into the open space between the tables and the bench dragging the hose of a vacuum-duster. Ahmed Khadra ducked under a table and tried to get it away from them. This was wonderful; screaming in delight, they all laid hold of the other end, and Mike and Mitzi and Superego and Complex ran to help them. The seven of them dragged Khadra about ten feet before he gave up and let go. At the same time, an incipient fight broke out on the other side of the arc of tables between the head of the language department at Mallorysport Academy and a spinsterish amateur phoneticist. At this point, Judge Pendarvis, deciding that if you can't prevent it, relax and enjoy it, rapped a few times with his gavel, and announced that court was recessed.

"You will all please remain here; this is not an adjournment, and if any of the various groups who seem to be discussing different aspects of the problem reach any conclusion they feel should be presented in evidence, will they please notify the bench so that court can be reconvened. In any case, we will reconvene at eleven thirty."

Somebody wanted to know if smoking would be permitted during the recess. The Chief Justice said that it would. He got out a cigar and lit it. Mamma Fuzzy wanted a puff: she didn't like it. Out of the corner of his eye, he saw Mike and Mitzi, Fora and Fauna scampering around and up the steps behind the bench. When he looked again, they were all up on it, and Mitzi was showing the court what she had in her shoulder bag.

He got up, with Mamma and Baby, and crossed to where Leslie Coombes was sitting. By this time, somebody was bringing in a coffee urn from the cafeteria. Fuzzies ought to happen oftener in court.

The gavel tapped slowly. Little Fuzzy scrambled up onto Jack Holloway's lap. After five days in court, they had all learned that the gavel meant for Fuzzies and other people to be quiet. It might be a good idea, Jack thought, to make a little gavel, when he got home, and keep it on the table in the living room for when the family got too boisterous. Baby, who wasn't gavel-trained yet, started out onto the floor; Mamma dashed after him and brought him back under the table.

The place looked like a courtroom again. The tables were ranged in a neat row facing the bench, and the witness chair and the jury box were back where they belonged. The ashtrays and the coffee urn and the ice tubs for beer and soft drinks had vanished. It looked like the party was over. He was almost regretful; it had been fun. Especially for seventeen Fuzzies and a Baby Fuzzy and a little black-and-white kitten.

There was one unusual feature; there was now a fourth man on the bench, in gold-braided Navy black; sitting a little apart from the judges, trying to look as though he weren't there at all—Space Commodore Alex Napier.

Judge Pendarvis laid down his gavel. "Ladies and gentlemen, are you ready to present the opinions you have reached?" he asked.

Lieutenant Ybarra, the Navy psychologist, rose. There was a reading screen in front of him; he snapped it on.

"Your Honors," he began, "there still exists considerable difference of opinion on matters of detail but we are in agreement on all major points. This is quite a lengthy report, and it has already been incorporated into the permanent record. Have I the court's permission to summarize it?"

The court told him he had. Ybarra glanced down at the screen in front of him and continued:

"It is our opinion," he said, "that sapients may be defined as differing from nonsapience in that it is characterized by conscious thought, by ability to think in logical sequence and by ability to think in terms other than mere sense data. We—meaning every member of every sapient

166

race—think consciously, and we know what we are thinking. This is not to say that all our mental activity is conscious. The science of psychology is based, to a large extent, upon our realization that only a small portion of our mental activity occurs above the level of consciousness, and for centuries we have been diagraming the mind as an iceberg, one-tenth exposed and nine-tenths submerged. The art of psychiatry consists largely in bringing into consciousness some of the content of this submerged nine-tenths, and as a practitioner I can testify to its difficulty and uncertainty.

"We are so habituated to conscious thought that when we reach some conclusion by any nonconscious process, we speak of it as a 'hunch,' or an 'intuition,' and question its validity. We are so habituated to acting upon consciously formed decisions that we must laboriously acquire, by systematic drill, those automatic responses upon which we depend for survival in combat or other emergencies. And we are by nature so unaware of this vast submerged mental area that it was not until the first century Pre-Atomic that its existence was more than vaguely suspected, and its nature is still the subject of acrimonious professional disputes."

There had been a few of those, off and on, during the past four days, too.

"If we depict sapient mentation as an iceberg, we might depict nonsapient mentation as the sunlight reflected from its surface. This is a considerably less exact analogy; while the nonsapient mind deals, consciously, with nothing but present sense data, there is a considerable absorption and re-emission of subconscious memories. Also, there are occasional flashes of what must be conscious mental activity, in dealing with some novel situation. Dr. van Riebeek, who is especially interested in the evolutionary aspect of the question, suggests that the introduction of novelty because of drastic environmental changes may have forced nonsapient beings into more or less sustained conscious thinking and so initiated mental habits which, in time, gave rise to true sapience.

"The sapient mind not only thinks consciously by habit, but it thinks in connected sequence. It associates one thing with another. It reasons logically, and forms conclusions, and uses those conclusions as premises from which to arrive at further conclusions. It groups associations together, and generalizes. Here we pass completely beyond any comparison with nonsapience. This is not merely more consciousness, or more thinking; it is thinking of a radically different kind. The nonsapient mind deals exclusively with crude sensory material. The sapient mind translates sense impressions into ideas, and then forms ideas *of* ideas, in ascending orders of abstraction, almost without limit.

"This, finally, brings us to one of the recognized overt manifestations of sapience. The sapient being is a symbol user. The nonsapient being cannot symbolize, because the nonsapient mind is incapable of concepts beyond mere sense images."

Ybarra drank some water, and twisted the dial of his reading screen with the other hand.

"The sapient being," he continued, "can do one other thing. It is a combination of the three abilitites already enumerated, but combining them creates something much greater than the mere sum of the parts. The sapient being can imagine. He can conceive of something which has no existence whatever in the sense-available world of reality, and then he can work and plan toward making it a part of reality. He can not only imagine, but he can also create."

He paused for a moment. "This is our definition of sapience. When we encounter any being whose mentation includes these characteristics, we may know him for a sapient brother. It is the considered opinion of all of us that the beings called Fuzzies are such beings."

Jack hugged the small sapient one on his lap, and Little Fuzzy looked up and murmured, *"He-inta?"*

"You're in, kid," he whispered. "You just joined the people."

Ybarra was saying, "They think consciously and continuously. We know that by instrumental analysis of their electroencephalographic patterns, which compare closely to those of an intelligent human child of ten. They think in connected sequence; I invite consideration of all the different logical steps involved in the invention, designing and making of their prawn-killing weapons, and in the development of tools with which to make them. We have abundant evidence of their ability to think beyond present sense data, to associate, to generalize, to abstract and to symbolize.

"And above all, they can imagine, not only a new implement, but a new way of life. We see this in the first human contact with the race which, I submit, should be designated as *Fuzzy sapiens.* Little Fuzzy found a strange and wonderful place in the forest, a place unlike anything he had ever seen, in which lived a powerful being. He imagined himself living in this place, enjoying the friendship and protection of this mysterious being. So he slipped inside, made friends with Jack Holloway and lived with him. And then he imagined his family sharing this precious comfort and companionship with him, and he went and found them and brought them back with him. Like so many other sapient beings, Little Fuzzy had a beautiful dream; like a fortunate few, he made it real."

The Chief Justice allowed the applause to run on for a few minutes before using his gavel to silence it. There was a brief colloquy among the three judges, and then the Chief Justice rapped again. Little Fuzzy looked perplexed. Everybody had been quiet after he did it the first time, hadn't they?

"It is the unanimous decision of the court to accept the report already entered into the record and just summarized by Lieutenant Ybarra, TFN, and to thank him and all who have been associated with him.

"It is now the ruling of this court that the species known as *Fuzzy fuzzy holloway zarathustra* is in fact a race of sapient beings, entitled to the respect of all other sapient beings and to the full protection of the law of the Terran Federation." He rapped again, slowly, pounding the decision into the legal framework.

Space Commodore Napier leaned over and whispered; all three of the judges nodded emphatically. The naval officer rose.

"Lieutenant Ybarra, on behalf of the Service and of the Federation, I thank you and those associated with you for a lucid and excellent report, the culmination of work which reflects credit upon all who participated in it. I also wish to state that a suggestion made to me by Lieutenant Ybarra regarding possible instrumental detection of sapient mentation is being credited to him in my own report, with

169

the recommendation that it be given important priority by the Bureau of Research and Development. Perhaps the next time we find people who speak beyond the range of human audition, who have fur and live in a mild climate, and who like their food raw, we'll know what they are from the beginning."

Bet Ybarra gets another stripe, and a good job out of this. Jack hoped so. Then Pendarvis was pounding again.

"I had almost forgotten; this is a criminal trial," he confessed. "It is the verdict of this court that the defendant, Jack Holloway, is not guilty as here charged. He is herewith discharged from custody. If he or his attorney will step up here, the bail bond will be refunded." He puzzled Little Fuzzy by hammering again with his gavel to adjourn court.

This time, instead of keeping quiet, everybody made all the noise they could, and Uncle Gus was holding him high over his head and shouting:

"The *winnah!* By unanimous decision!"

XVII

Ruth Ortheris sipped at the tart, cold cocktail. It was good; oh, it was good, all good! The music was soft, the lights were dim, the tables were far apart; just she and Gerd, and nobody was paying any attention to them. And she was clear out of the business, too. An agent who testified in court always was expended in service like a fired round. They'd want her back, a year from now, to testify when the board of inquiry came out from Terra, but she wouldn't be Lieutenant j.g. Ortheris then, she'd be Mrs. Gerd van Riebeek. She set down the glass and rubbed the sunstone on her finger. It was a lovely sunstone, and it meant such a lovely thing.

And we're getting married with a ready-made family, too. Four Fuzzies and a black-and-white kitten.

"You're sure you really want to go to Beta?" Gerd asked. "When Napier gets this new government organized, it'll be taking over Science Center. We could both get our old jobs back. Maybe something better."

"You don't want to go back?" He shook his head. "Neither do I. I want to go to Beta and be a sunstone digger's wife."

"And a Fuzzyolgist."

"And a Fuzzyologist. I couldn't drop that now. Gerd, we're only beginning with them. We know next to nothing about their psychology."

He nodded seriously. "You know, they may turn out to be even wiser than we are."

She laughed. "Oh, Gerd! Let's don't get too excited about them. Why, they're just like little children. All they think about is having fun."

"That's right. I said they were wiser than we are. They stick to important things." He smoked silently for a moment. "It's not just their psychology; we don't know anything much about their physiology, or biology either." He picked up his glass and drank. "Here, we had eighteen of them in all. Seventeen adults and one little one. Now what kind of ratio is that? And the ones we saw in the woods ran about the same. In all, we sighted about a hundred and fifty adults and only ten children."

"Maybe last year's crop have grown up," she began.

"You know any other sapient races with a one-year maturation period?" he asked. "I'll bet they take ten or fifteen years to mature. Jack's Baby Fuzzy hasn't gained a pound in the last month. And another puzzle; this craving for Extee Three. That's not a natural food; except for the cereal bulk matter, it's purely synthetic. I was talking to Ybarra; he was wondering if there mightn't be something in it that caused an addiction."

"Maybe it satisfies some kind of dietary deficiency."

"Well, we'll find out." He inverted the jug over his glass. "Think we could stand another cocktail before dinner?"

Space Commodore Napier sat at the desk that had been Nick Emmert's and looked at the little man with the red whiskers and the rumpled suit, who was looking back at him in consternation.

"Good Lord, Commodore; you can't be serious?"

"But I am. Quite serious, Dr. Rainsford."

"Then you're nuts!" Rainsford exploded. "I'm no more qualified to be Governor General than I'd be to command Xerxes Base. Why, I never held an administrative position in my life."

"That might be a recommendation. You're replacing a veteran administrator."

"And I have a job. The Institute of Zeno-Sciences—"

"I think they'll be glad to give you leave, under the circumstances. Doctor, you're the logical man for this job. You're an ecologist; you know how disastrous the effects of upsetting the balance of nature can be. The Zarathustra Company took care of this planet, when it was their property, but now nine-tenths of it is public domain, and people will be coming in from all over the Federation, scrambling to get rich overnight. You'll know how to control things."

"Yes, as Commissioner of Conservation, or something I'm qualified for."

"As Governor General. Your job will be to make policy. You can appoint the administrators."

"Well, who, for instance?"

"Well, you're going to need an Attorney General right away. Who will you appoint for that position?"

"Gus Brannhard," Rainsford said instantly.

"Good. And who—this question is purely rhetorical—will you appoint as Commissioner of Native Affairs?"

Jack Holloway was going back to Beta Continent on the constabulary airboat. Official passenger: Mr. Commissioner Jack Holloway. And his staff: Little Fuzzy, Mamma Fuzzy, Baby Fuzzy, Mike, Mitzi, Ko-Ko and Cinderella. Bet they didn't know they had official positions!

Somehow he wished he didn't have one himself.

"Want a good job, George?" he asked Lunt.

"I have a good job."

"This'll be a better one. Rank of major, eighteen thousand a year. Commandant, Native Protection Force. And you won't lose seniority in the constabulary; Colonel Ferguson'll give you indefinite leave."

"Well, cripes, Jack, I'd like to, but I don't want to leave the kids. And I can't take them away from the rest of the gang."

"Bring the rest of the gang along. I'm authorized to borrow twenty men from the constabulary as a training cadre, and you only have sixteen. Your sergeants'll get commissions, and all your men will be sergeants. I'm going to have a force of a hundred and fifty for a start."

"You must think the Fuzzies are going to need a lot of protection."

"They will. The whole country between the Cordilleras and the West Coast Range will be Fuzzy Reservation and that'll have to be policed. Then the Fuzzies outside that will have to be protected. You know what's going to happen. Everybody wants Fuzzies; why, even Judge Pendarvis approached me about getting a pair for his wife. There'll be gangs hunting them to sell, using stun-bombs and sleep-gas and everything. I'm going to have to set up an adoption bureau; Ruth will be in charge of that. And that'll mean a lot of investigators—"

Oh, it was going to be one hell of a job! Fifty thousand

173

a year would be chicken feed to what he'd lose by not working his diggings. But somebody would have to do it, and the Fuzzies were his responsibility.

Hadn't he gone to law to prove their sapience?

They were going home, home to the Wonderful Place. They had seen many wonderful places, since the night they had been put in the bags: the place where everything had been light and they had been able to jump so high and land so gently, and the place where they had met all the others of their people and had so much fun. But now they were going back to the old Wonderful Place in the woods, where it had all started.

And they had met so many Big Ones, too. Some Big Ones were bad, but only a few; most Big Ones were good. Even the one who had done the killing had felt sorry for what he had done; they were all sure of that. And the other Big Ones had taken him away, and they had never seen him again.

He had talked about that with the others—with Flora and Fauna, and Dr. Crippen, and Complex, and Superego, and Dillinger and Lizzie Borden. Now that they were all going to live with the Big Ones, they would have to use those funny names. Someday they would find out what they meant, and that would be fun, too. And they could; now the Big Ones could put things in their ears and hear what they were saying, and Pappy Jack was learning some of their words, and teaching them some of his.

And soon all the people would find Big Ones to live with, who would take care of them and have fun with them and love them, and give them the Wonderful Food. And with the Big Ones taking care of them, maybe more of their babies would live and not die so soon. And they would pay the Big Ones back. First they would give their love and make them happy. Later, when they learned how, they would give their help, too.

MORE SCIENCE FICTION ADVENTURE!